TempestFray

The Storm Begins

Scott Strozier

Publisher's Note:

This is a work of fiction. All names, characters, places, and events are the work of the author's imagination.

Any resemblance to real persons, places, or events is coincidental.

Solstice Publishing -
www.solsticepublishing.com

Prologue

This sixteenth day of September in the year of our Lord one thousand eight hundred and fifty-six marks the one-year anniversary of the destruction of the Albatross. In this time of peace it is truly hard to fathom that a little over a year ago the entire world was gripped by fear. The armies, navies, and leaders of the world brought to their knees by one man...Robur the Conqueror.

Who was this man? Where did he come from? Even after extensive research, we still know so little of this man. What we do know is that he was a genius who designed and built a machine to master the skies above. A massive apparatus just a little smaller than a frigate but able to move through the air like a falcon. The ship was a miracle of technology the likes of which will not be surpassed for many years, decades even.

He could have sold this amazing machine, any country in the world would have paid the Albatross' weight in gold for just the design. But Robur did not want gold, he did not want fame, I don't believe he wanted recognition. No, what he desired most was a world without war and the Albatross was built to accomplish just that. A noble ambition you might say, and it was, and for Robur it was an ambition that must be achieved at all costs.

What should have been a great symbol of human ingenuity, an inspiration for the human race to soar to new heights, became the unstoppable weapon of a madman. For his ambition, for his world without war, Robur would force the world into peace. He used the Albatross to fly above the nations of the world, calling down to them with some sort voice amplifier.

"Disband your armies, disband your navies!" he called out.

To no avail, the countries that did not laugh turned their weapons upon the Albatross. They might as well have tried to hit the sun as the rounds from their cannons never made it halfway to Robur's great ship. This was when those armies realized Robur's words were not a statement but a command. Before anyone knew what was happening the warships began to explode, another of Robur's marvels, incendiary devices that detonated on contact engulfing the ships in flames. They never stood a chance...

For months this continued, Robur would call to the nations to disband their armies, they would refuse and death would rain down upon them. Every nation, every country big or small, was visited. All tried to resist...all failed. High above the clouds Robur could not be touched, the Albatross seemed truly invincible. So how? How was it that Robur the Conqueror the self-proclaimed master of the world was finally stopped?

All the weapons of all the nations of the world were powerless; in the end Robur's downfall was four stubborn stowaways, an ammunitions manufacturer going by the name Uncle Prudent, his daughter Dorothy Prudent, Phillip Evans, and U.S. government agent John Strock. Three men and one woman succeeded where the entire world failed. How you might ask? If you can believe it, entirely by accident.

Their story started before Robur's terror from the sky, with strange lights and Bible verses being heard from a dormant volcano. Naturally this caused a panic, which is where our four heroes enter. The

American agent approached Uncle Prudent at the Weldon Institute, a flight-enthusiast club, while he was introducing his new balloon. Mr. Strock asked Uncle Prudent for use of his hot air balloon to investigate the sounds coming from the dormant volcano. Uncle Prudent agreed as long as his daughter and Mr. Evans could accompany him on the maiden voyage. I can only assume that Mr. Strock thought it all a wild hoax for he agreed without protest.

They began their ascent the moment they arrived in town, which has requested to be anonymous. Even our heroes are not certain about what exactly happened next, all they can really remember is a large amount of smoke followed by strange sounds, explosions, and their balloon falling into the volcano. Next thing our heroes knew, they were waking up in a locked cabin aboard the Albatross. They were with Robur as he flew across the world, as he threatened the nations and as he delivered on his threats.

Why Robur kept them on board is hard to say, our four heroes have remained strangely silent on the matter. Perhaps he wanted an audience, maybe he wanted some sort of validation for his actions, who knows? Whatever the reason may have been the world is now safe because of it.

Although our heroes were allowed to walk freely upon the ship they were closely watched and confined to the lower decks whenever the Albatross came upon a new city. After months of being imprisoned a quirk of fate gave them the opportunity they needed to destroy the Albatross.

In the Arabian Desert Robur swooped down to stop a tribal war, dropping bombs upon the two armies. During this display of power the Albatross came too low and was caught in the blast of his own explosive devices. The Albatross was damaged enough to require the ship to be anchored to a nearby beach while the crew made repairs. Our heroes saw their chance; with the crew scurrying around to fix the damaged ship, no one was paying much attention to the four stowaways.

They moved through the ship dodging the crew members and made it to the armory where the chemicals for Robur's explosives were stored. Mr. Strock was able to construct a crude fuse to give them time to get away from Albatross before it exploded. They used the anchor to get off the ship with crewman firing from above and cut the line once they were on the ground. The ship soared away and before they could turn around the armory exploded and the mighty Albatross was engulfed in flames. Our heroes watched as the ship crashed into the sea.

And so ended the reign of the Master of the World, perhaps the greatest technological mind of our time, outsmarted by four stowaways. Robur and his ship were never found, even after an extensive search; there have been rumors of sightings here and there but nothing confirmed. A year passed and still we keep a watchful eye on skies above afraid of being in the shadow of the Albatross. Are we just being paranoid? Is this simply the eye of the storm? Or can we simply not accept that a man who brought the world to its knees could be stopped?

Perhaps putting these fears to rest is as simple as accepting that this is the one-year anniversary of the Destruction of the Albatross.

Chapter One
The Oncoming Storm

There are many uncharted and undiscovered islands in the world. Most find this fact surprising, we look at maps and we believe that every corner of the world has been seen and recorded. Therefore, it would probably surprise people just how vast the oceans of the world are, how many islands remain off the maps. An uncharted island is where our storm begins with a young man walking barefoot along the beach. A man named Bryant, who is about six feet tall wearing a simple white shirt and brown pants, walks along the white sands ignoring the ocean waves and lush green trees. Bryant stares ahead moving towards the base of the mountain covered in flowered foliage. When he reaches the face of the wall, he pulls on a blue flower to have the side of the mountain open.

Before the mountainside opens completely he enters and looks up at the mighty structure. The airship is a dull silver color with brass bindings along its sides. It is similar to the shape of a submarine save that it is a bit wider and not as long. The top of the ship has a wooden deck stretching to the flight cabin and two large exhaust ports at the ship's end. There is a base cabin at the bottom of the airship where Bryant walks up to a large metal door bearing an extravagant embroidered 'A' on it. There is a strange handle on the door which Bryant takes hold of, twisting it to the right then left and right again.

The door opens quickly allowing Bryant to enter a room similar to an airlock with brass dials and incomplete displays on the right side of the room. To the left is an open doorway where a Victorian styled spiral staircase can be seen. Bryant heads straight for this staircase and ascends four floors up into the airship, and enters a large engine room. The floor is a steel grating covering cables of all sizes running to large device similar to a nuclear reactor with a steampunk design to it.

The sound of mechanical tools at work can be heard as he enters, but there is no sign of its source. Bryant searches the engine room looking for the source of the sound as it continues to echo thru the room.

"Ryland? You in here?" Bryant finally calls out looking back and forth through the room.

"Yeah. Just finishing up some modifications," Ryland calls out standing up from beneath a panel he has been working on.

He is a tall lean man dressed in a Victorian style vest with a white button-down shirt with the sleeves rolled up. Ryland puts down his tools and walks over to a panel and begins turning dials and pushing buttons. Bryant walks up behind him looking curiously at the panel. After a few moments Ryland turns to Bryant.

"You're just in time. I finished installing the software and hardware for the new interface control system, now we just have to hope it works," Ryland says before turning back to the panel.

He pulls a lever very slowly towards him. Lights on the panel begin to flash as both men look with anticipation around the room. The entire engine room begins to come to life. Through mechanized sounds and electrical equipment turning on a computerized voice breaks in.

"Cyber Interactive Control System is now online, primary ship's diagnostics check now underway," the automated voice says.

A wide grin spreads across Ryland's face as Bryant bursts into laughter patting him on the shoulder.

"It works! It really works!" Bryant exclaims proudly as he looks around the room.

Ryland looks at Bryant with a pleased smile on his face.

"You doubted me?" he asks, arms extending to the rest of the ship.

Bryant smirks at his friend's sarcastic joke, crossing his arms as he leans on one of the panels.

"Only because I know you," he says.

"And what exactly is that supposed to mean?" Ryland asks crossing his arms in turn.

Bryant lightly shakes his head before standing up straight putting his hands in his pockets and taking a few steps closer to Ryland.

"Oh let's see. There was the breakfast robot that tried to scramble us, the rocket-powered speedboat that launched into orbit. Oh and who can forget—" Bryant lists off clearly enjoying it.

"Okay, okay stop right there," Ryland interrupts uncrossing his arms.

"I was twelve and younger when I built those, my knowledge of technology was a little lacking, but since then there have been no mishaps," he defends again crossing his arms.

Bryant stares at his friend skeptically, hands in his pockets, rocking back and forth on his heels.

"None?" he asks.

"Well, no major ones..." Ryland replies rather sheepishly. "Did you come here for some purpose other than to remind me of my shortcomings?" A bit annoyed he walks towards the spiral staircase.

Bryant lightly chuckles at his friend's last statement before following after him.

"Well that is a fulltime job; but yes actually, I wanted to see how the repairs were going and ask...what exactly are they for?"

Ryland stops, and turning to Bryant he gestures to the whole room.

"Well the C.I.C.S. will enable me to control the Albatross singlehandedly without the need of the thirty-man crew it originally required. Also the C.I.C.S. is programed with security protocols that will prevent anyone but myself from piloting the ship. She is mine, and the C.I.C.S. will make sure she stays that way," he explains.

"Never pegged you as the possessive type," Bryant quips.

"Funny…" Ryland says in a deadpan tone. "You know the power of this ship. You know what it could do in the 1800s with its primitive technology. Now that I have had a go at it, this ship is more dangerous than ever." He continues to walk to the staircase.

"This way the ship remains in my hands and safe from madmen who would use it to conquer the world…again," he says proceeding down the staircase.

"It also prevents four stowaways from sabotaging the ship and destroying it," Bryant says following after Ryland.

Ryland looks back at his friend a bit annoyed at the last remark.

"That is not the purpose of the system," Ryland exclaims as he reaches the bottom of the staircase.

"Yeah I know. I'm just saying you've learned from your great-great-grandfather's mistake," Bryant answers as he too reaches the bottom of the staircase.

"His mistake was his whole reason for building the Albatross, he was insane," Ryland says proceeding toward the door.

"Was he?"

Ryland immediately stops and turns to face his friend.

"What?" he asks.

"Was he rely insane? He wanted a world without war, without conflict, a world of peace; is that so crazy?" Ryland stares at Bryant with a bewildered look on his face.

"The dream was not crazy, it was how he went about it, he bombed entire armies and navies, he slaughtered thousands!" Ryland exclaims.

"In order to save everyone!" Bryant counters. "Maybe he understood the world better than all of us, force is used to suppress the weak, and force is the drive of conflict. Maybe force is all the world really understands.

"What if he was right? Perhaps the only hope for peace is to force it upon the world," he finishes taking a step closer to Ryland.

"You can't force peace on the world!" Ryland shouts.

"As long as there are people they will always have a reason to fight," he counters.

"Besides one man can't be the moral compass of the world. My great-great-grandfather proved that."

"No he didn't; he was stopped. His plan was derailed before he ever had the chance to complete it…" Bryant counters stepping closer to Ryland.

"And what?" Ryland asks. "You think it would have worked? The American on his ship was there to stop him, if it hadn't been him it would have been another, they would have fought back; one man cannot stand up to the whole world and hope to win," Ryland tells him.

"One man can change the course of history, and one man with a powerful machine brought the world to its knees...imagine what two could accomplish." Bryant holds up two fingers.

"Two men?" Ryland asks clearly confused. "One more person will not make a difference; Robur had an entire crew with him, he was still stopped," he says in a matter of fact tone.

"No, no, not two men; two machines," Bryant responds with an unwavering gaze.

"Machines?" Ryland asks.

"The Albatross...and the Nautilus," Bryant replies causing Ryland's eyes to open wide.

"The Nautilus?" Ryland asks clearly confused. "Nemo's ship was lost; it has been for over a hundred years."

"Yes, but what if it were found? Think about it; the Albatross and the Nautilus!" Excitement is growing in Bryant's voice. "The two greatest technological achievements ever conceived by men! Together the ships master both sky and sea and therefore control the earth. From sea and sky the world could be—"

"Could be what?" Ryland interrupts. "Forced to like each other? Forced to get along? Have you learned nothing from the stories of this ship? The world can't be forced into peace. These machines are just that, machines!" he says anger evident in his voice. "They do not make us gods! They don't give us the right to dictate even one single person, let alone the world! It's a good dream; but it's just that…a dream. And one that should be abandoned for more practical goals," Ryland finishes trying to regain his composure.

Bryant backs off, realizing he has upset his friend.

"I guess you have a point. I'm sorry Ryland, it's just… this ship is amazing! How can you stand never using it? Having it just sit here? Don't you wish it could be used for…something?" Bryant asks trying to calm his friend.

"Perhaps one day it can be…but until I feel the world is ready it will stay here, invisible to the outside world."

Bryant doesn't say anything but lightly nods in agreement. Ryland's eyes soften and he reaches out to his friend.

"It will never work you know…" Ryland pats Bryant on the shoulder.

"Forcing world peace; it will never work, best just forget about it and find another goal to shoot for…something that can actually be accomplished," Ryland says in a comforting voice, removing his hand from Bryant's shoulder.

"Yeah, it was just a passing thought…you know?" Bryant responds.

"Right, of course I mean like I said the Nautilus has been lost for over a century, it's not like it's been found…right Bryant?" Ryland asks.

"Right; Captain Nemo's Nautilus is lost and it doesn't look like it will be uncovered anytime soon. Probably for the best," Bryant says in a deadpan tone.

"Probably," Ryland answers.

Chapter Two
The Storm Reaches the Shore

Six years go by since the conversation between Bryant and Ryland. On a military base in Connecticut the atmosphere is relaxed with soldiers in groups talking and goofing off after the daily training has been completed. Some are playing football, some are eating, none have their guns at the ready and few are in full uniform. On this uneventful day three of these soldiers will be forced into a conflict they never prepared for. Private Alexandria 'Alex' Lawson, a slender woman with short auburn hair and green eyes, watches a makeshift football game with Private Marcus Samuels. Marcus is just under six feet with short black hair and a friendly face. Alex sighs before turning to talk to Marcus.

"Another leisure day, and to think when I joined the army my parents were afraid I would be in danger," she says shaking her head. "So far the only danger here is boredom."

"Yeah I know what you mean," Marcus answers. "I thought I would get to see all the latest weapons and tools, instead I have been learning how to scrub more efficiently." He makes a scrubbing motion with both hands.

Alex smiles and nods at Marcus's comment before returning their attention to the game as one-side scores a touchdown. During their conversation, they did not notice the approach of one of the few soldiers in full uniform. He is as tall as Marcus and in his late forties, carrying himself with an air of command. His face is expressionless as he addresses the two oblivious soldiers.

"So life on the base is too quiet for you?" Colonel Winters asks.

Startled, Alex and Marcus quickly rise, saluting as they face the colonel at attention.

"Sir!" they say in unison.

"At ease." Alex and Marcus put their arms down.

"The army is not about excitement," Colonel Winters says grabbing their attention. "It's about being there when your country needs you. A soldier's responsibility is to be where they are needed in order to protect its citizens. So if you're here for glory you might as well—"

Colonel Winter's speech is interrupted by an explosion destroying a building of the base behind Marcus and Alex. All three instinctively duck and head for cover trying to assess what is going on. The air erupts with sounds of guns firing and soldiers running, sounds of orders to fire. Alex, Colonel Winters, and Marcus are trying to make it to the munitions. Running they see other soldiers being pushed back; one of the soldiers closest to Marcus is struck and he hits the ground with electricity arcing over his body. More explosions erupt as buildings on the base including the munitions they were heading for erupting into flames. The few soldiers with guns keep firing through smoke on unseen attackers.

With no guns to get a hold of, Alex, Marcus, and Colonel Winters rush to a destroyed building and take cover. They look out to see more of the U.S. soldiers fall with electricity arcing over their bodies. As the attackers emerge from the smoke, Alex's eyes widen at the sight of strange soldiers wearing a steampunk styled underwater breathing apparatus. It is over a long blue coat with ornate silver colored bits of armor attached.

The weapons they carry are guns that appear to be from the 1800s covered with ornate brass colored parts at the center. She gets quick glances at other strangely ornate Victorian styled weapons that are destroying the base around them.

The battle is quick and save for Alex, Marcus, and Colonel Winters the American soldiers are all dead. Breathing heavily behind the ruined wall where they are hiding Marcus and Alex look at Colonel Winters.

"Alright, we need to try to warn someone," he says trying to keep his composure. "If we can get to the base headquarters we should be able to call for help."

"But wouldn't they have already called for help?" Alex interjects. "Plus that, whoever these guys are they're well trained. Wouldn't they have disabled our communications?" she asks trying to keep her voice down.

"She's right, these guys came out of nowhere and in force," Marcus says to the colonel. "Which means they must have disabled our early detection systems. Colonel I have seen those systems, that's no easy task, it shouldn't even be possible."

"Then what are we going to—" Alex begins.

She is interrupted as one of the aquatic steampunk soldiers appears behind them aiming his electric Victorian weapon at them.

"You three stand up! Guns down, and hands where I can see them!" the aquatic soldier shouts.

The three of them raise their hands to show they have no guns as they slowly stand and face the soldier.

"Alright now move!" he says gesturing the direction with his gun.

They are moved into the open where several more of the aquatic soldiers are standing. Once in the open one of the soldiers approaches the first soldier.

"What is this?" the second soldier asks.

"Found them hiding in the building. Survivors, sir."

"You heard the captain. There are no survivors," the second soldier says. "Take care of it." He turns and walks away.

"Yes sir! Alright you three over there now!" he commands gesturing with his gun.

Alex, Marcus, and Colonel Winters are moved over to a vacant space as the aquatic soldier is joined by a few others who aim their weapons and prepare to fire.

"Aim!" the aquatic soldier shouts.

But before the soldiers can fire an electrical charging sound is heard. A figure appears out of the rubble of a nearby building wielding a Victorian styled dish weapon. The dish weapon fires and bolts of electricity suddenly erupt from the electric Victorian guns causing the soldiers to throw them to the ground. In one quick motion the stranger then puts away his dish weapon and comes into full view. He is wearing a double-breasted navy-blue coat, light grey pants with knee high boots, and a biker's helmet.

He rushes at the aquatic soldiers wielding a steampunk single-stick weapon that is arcing electricity. The soldiers are still stunned and attempt to fight back in vain but the stranger takes them down easily. He turns to the three American soldiers for a brief moment before turning back to fight the aquatic steampunk soldiers.

"Don't just stand there, run!" he tells them.

They don't need to be told twice as they run for the ruins of the building that the stranger first emerged from. The commotion has brought more of the aquatic soldiers to the position. The helmeted man redraws his dish weapon and aims it at the oncoming soldiers. The soldiers' weapons again arc electricity forcing them to discard them. Instead of rushing towards them he turns and rushes past our trio and heads to the other end of the military base.

"Hey wait! Where are you going?!" Alex yells after him.

She gets no response as Marcus turns to run after the stranger.

"Come on!" he shouts back to Alex and the colonel.

"Marcus, where do you think you are going?" the colonel calls after him.

Marcus pauses but continues to move in the direction that the stranger has gone.

"I don't know about you, but I'm going to follow the person who can actually fight these guys!" Marcus responds following after the stranger.

"He makes sense sir," Alex says to the colonel before sprinting after them.

"Damn it, he does!" Colonel Winters yells as he too follows.

The three American soldiers rush after the stranger, he is not far ahead and they see him dash into a slightly damaged building. Rushing in after him they find him at the only working computer with a flash drive device plugged into the working terminal. On the computer screen there is displayed a progress bar with a download nearly complete. Cautiously and trying to sound commanding Colonel Winters approaches the stranger.

"What do you think you're doing?" he asks to no avail.

"Look I don't know who you are, but those computers are the property of the—" the colonel begins again.

Before the colonel can finish the download completes. Without a word the stranger takes the flash drive device out of the terminal and then immediately runs out of the building, not paying any attention to the three Americans.

Before they can protest, the sound of the aquatic soldiers' guns are heard again and without a second thought the trio quickly run after the stranger managing to catch up with him as shots are fired behind them. He leads them off the base, every now and again turning briefly to use his dish weapon and disable the aquatic soldiers' weapons. Alex manages to catch up to the stranger.

"Hey, where are we going? There is nothing out here!" she yells at the stranger without getting a response.

"Hey! Did you hear me?"

The stranger continues to run toward the outskirts of the base, ignoring Alex and the others, as the aquatic soldiers gain on them. Just as they reach the outskirts the stranger pulls out a cell phone and begins typing furiously. Soon the phone responds.

"Exterior defenses, 30 second delay initiate," a voice comes from the phone.

"Defenses! What defenses?" Marcus asks.

"There's nothing out..." Alex begins.

Alex, Colonel Winters, and Marcus stop dead in their tracks as a massive airship seems to just appear right in front of them. They stare for a moment in fascination at the airship, however the stranger does not miss a step as he rushes to a door on the side of the ship. Quickly manipulating the turn lock he opens the door before rushing in.

On the airship's exterior sounds of electrical charging erupt from all over the ship as mechanized laser like devices appear on the airship's sides. As the weapons begin to take aim at the approaching aquatic soldiers the trio manage to snap out of their fascinated daze and rush into the now open door of the airship. They make it inside just before the door automatically closes.

Arcs of electricity shoot from the airship's exterior as the weapons begin taking down the aquatic soldiers. Electrical pulses hit the soldiers and erupt in a burst of electricity throwing the soldiers back a couple of feet. Ten of the soldiers are taken down by these weapons and they quickly learn they are outmatched halting their advance and turning to run.

Inside the airship our trio land on the grated floor as the door closes shut behind them. Breathing heavily they start looking around the Victorian styled airlock they have just entered.

"Where…where did this come from?" Marcus asks still breathing heavily.

"Never mind where, what is this thing?" Colonel Winters responds.

While the three of them are taking in their surroundings the stranger is at the other side of the room manipulating another lock. Still ignoring the three soldiers he opens the door revealing a Victorian spiral staircase and immediately ascends.

"Hey wait! Where are you going?" Alex shouts at the departing stranger.

Alex follows the stranger up the stairs followed by Marcus and Colonel Winters. He continues to ignore the three soldiers chasing after him, still typing furiously at his phone. Alex speeds up still trying to talk to the stranger.

"Wait! Please stop!" she implores. "Who are you?! Please just talk to us…"

"Wait…stop! We just want to talk," Marcus calls out from behind Alex.

"Stop! What's going on?" Colonel Winters shouts.

"What is this?" Marcus shouts. "Are you with the army?"

"Who were those soldiers? How did you…" Alex persists in spite of receiving no response.

The stranger continues to ignore the three American soldiers as he finally exits the stairway to a short hallway. He runs clear to the end of the hall through an open doorway with the Americans close behind still trying to get him to respond. The three of them immediately go silent as they enter what looks like a steampunk version of a naval ship with an ornate ship wheel in the center surrounded by controls and monitors. The room ends with a large observing window to look out upon the sky. The stranger puts away his phone and rushes to the ship's steering wheel immediately manipulating some of the controls.

"Computer begin ascent…and scan for reactor radiation field!" the stranger yells.

"Initiating ascent. Radiation field not detected," a computerized voice responds causing the three to look up and around the room.

"Keep scanning," he says still manipulating the controls. "Inform me immediately if the radiation field appears.

"Front starboard cameras on retreating soldiers display on diagnostic screen two," he orders still ignoring the Americans.

"Displaying now," the computerized voice responds.

The three Americans have not moved from the spot where they entered the room but their attention is drawn to one of the monitors around the captain's wheel as it suddenly displays a scene of the retreating aquatic soldiers. The airship suddenly lifts into the air causing the Americans to brace themselves on nearby control panels as the ship ascends and turns with surprising speed to pursue the strange soldiers. At the wheel the stranger is unaffected by the speed of the ship's movement.

Outside the retreating soldiers run toward a vehicle that has just arrived. The vehicle is bronze in color with eight wheels and exterior designs that look Indian in origin. The back of the vehicle opens up and six soldiers rush out of it to gather up the unconscious aquatic soldiers. The soldiers who are still standing rush past the others into the vehicle, the others get the unconscious aboard quickly. Once aboard the door to the vehicle does not even have a chance to close before the vehicle is off heading toward an empty harbor near the base. The vehicle is surprisingly fast but the airship is able to keep up with them.

Aboard the airship Marcus, Alex, and the colonel look out the large observatory window of the control room.

"Oh my God…we're…we're flying!" Marcus exclaims. "This…this…it's an airship!" he says turning to Alex and the colonel.

"What…no…no that's impossible…unless..." Colonel Winters mumbles to himself before turning to look toward the stranger at the wheel.

"Warning U.S. Air Force alerted to attack. Interception by American fighters imminent. Retreat advised," the computerized voice suddenly breaks in.

"Stay on the AquaMotive!" the stranger responds. "Begin tracking any foreign objects in the sky and display them on Screen One. Increase speed and begin prepping the Anti-Particle Bomb."

"Tracking American fighters, they will arrive in ten minutes. Anti-Particle Bomb charging now," the computerized voice answers.

Alex walks over to the stranger with the colonel following close behind as Marcus remains looking out the window. The stranger continues manipulating the wheel and other controls seemingly oblivious to their existence.

"Anti-Particle Bomb? What is that?" Alex asks him, still not getting a response.

"Those fighters are here to help us. We need to relay a message to them." Colonel Winters speaks directly to the stranger.

"Reactor radiation field detected ten miles ahead. American fighters will soon be in radar range," the computerized voice says.

"Jam all radar signals and engage electrostatic scrambler!" he shouts and moves to another control panel. "You're not getting away this time," he says to himself as he operates the control panel.

"Who? Who's not getting away?" Alex asks coming up to the stranger.

Still getting no response the colonel comes up next to the stranger and says in his most commanding voice, "Sir! As a colonel in the U.S. Armed Forces I demand to know what is going on! Now you will answer me!" he says in an obvious drill sergeant voice.

"Uh…guys you're going to want to see this," Marcus calls from the window.

Alex and Colonel Winters rush to see what Marcus is looking at. The AquaMobile can be seen heading up the dock where a large submarine is emerging from the water. The submarine is bronze in color with a steel deck on its top, the bow and stern of the submarine are decorated with elaborate Indian designs. As soon as the submarine is partway out of the water a side compartment is opened and a ramp is quickly lowered to the dock.

The AquaMobile travels up the ramp extending from the submarine and the ramp is retracted as soon as the vehicle is in the submarine. A compartment on the back of the submarine then opens up and a missile is launched.

In the control room the missile can be seen heading toward the airship causing the three soldiers to back away from the window.

They turn to the stranger but before any of them can speak, "Missile incoming," the computerized voice informs.

"Not going to be that easy," the stranger says as he flips a switch.

The Americans look out the observatory window where the missile can still be seen heading toward them. Before it can get too close a beam of light followed by an electric bolt strikes the incoming missile causing it to fall harmlessly to the ground. The trio stare in amazement while the stranger rushes toward the steering wheel.

"Prepare to launch Anti-Particle Bomb on my mark!" he calls out.

Just then alarms go off inside the control room followed by a sudden jolt rocking the airship and its four passengers to the floor.

"American fighters initiating attack. Suggest evasive maneuvers," the computerized voice says.

The stranger quickly gets off the ground and gets back to the steering wheel. Groaning, the three American soldiers get up as well.

"When I said track the fighters, I meant warn me before they attack!" he yells.

"Correction recorded for future reference," the computerized voice responds.

"Damn computer. Increase speed! I will not lose him again!" he responds working furiously at the controls next to the wheel.

Before the trio can even properly stand up they have to brace themselves as the airship picks up speed. The submarine is doing the same and beginning to dive. Two American fighters are attacking the airship and ignoring the submarine. They are firing missiles at the airship but the electrostatic field keeps detonating the missiles prematurely. Although the missiles are detonating away from the ship the concussive force is enough to rock the airship forcing the passengers to hold onto whatever they can in the control room.

"We have to open communications!" Colonel Winters shouts holding onto a nearby panel. "We have to tell the fighters they have the wrong target."

The colonel is ignored as concussive blasts continue to rock the airship.

"Computer, initiate soft-bigboy," the stranger suddenly yells.

"Initiating, in 5...4...3...2...1," the computerized voice responds.

At the bottom of the airship an ornate four-sided dish device descends from an open compartment. Once down the device emits a loud base-toned sound causing the fighters to suddenly pitch and begin to fly erratically. Marcus, who has managed to get back to the observatory window, stares at the scene with a mix of horror and fascination. He then steps away from the window and looks at the stranger.

"Those fighters! What...what did you do?" Marcus asks.

"Those were American fighters! They were on our side!" Colonel Winters shouts at the stranger.

"Are they…dead? Did you destroy those fighters?" Alex asks walking up next to the stranger.

"The soft-bigboy disables software of anything within a fifty-foot range. However, primary systems are left unharmed. The pilots will soon have complete control over their fighters. The soft-bigboy leaves no damage to aircraft or pilot, they are quite safe ma'am," the computerized voice suddenly answers her.

Alex looks up and around at the control room…

"Oh…good. Thanks?" she responds.

"You are welcome ma'am. Nautilus is now in range. Anti-Particle Bomb ready to deploy," the computerized voice says.

"At last; line up the Naut—" the stranger begins.

He is interrupted as the airship is suddenly rocked violently by an explosion outside sending the four of them crashing back to the floor. Alarms with flashing red lights go off and the stranger rushes over to another panel beginning to furiously turn knobs and push buttons.

"Damage to the lower decks has been sustained," the computer voice relays.

"I figured that!" the stranger says as he gets back on his feet.

"Damn weapon still doesn't work right," he says to himself. "Never mind; is the Nautilus locked on?" he asks working at another panel.

"Locked on," the computer voice responds.

"Fire!" he shouts turning a knob on the panel.

A light suddenly flashes on and off on the opposite panel.

"Anti-Particle Bomb had been disabled," the computer voice informs.

"No...*no!*" he yells as he rushes through the Americans to the opposite panel.

The ship is hit with another jolt but even the Americans manage to keep their footing this time around.

"Communications from fighters intercepted. They are requesting reinforcements," the computerized voice states.

The stranger, still wearing the biker helmet, looks out of the observatory window towards the sea before dropping his head for a few seconds. "Computer, track the Nautilus as long as possible," he says rushing back to the wheel. "Begin ascension and prepare flash Houdini."

The trio look at the stranger in confusion but say nothing realizing at this point that they would not get a response anyway. All three have more or less decided their best option is to stay out of his way until they are no longer under attack.

***

Outside the two American fighters come back around for another pass at the massive airship. Johnathan Renford and Gus Masters fly the two jets.

"Reinforcements are being deployed. Ten minutes. Gus we need to stall that ship until then," Johnathan says over the radio.

"Roger, preparing heat seekers—" Gus responds.

Gus is interrupted as he looks out of his cockpit to the airship as it seems to light up in a brilliant flash of light.

"What…what's…?" Johnathan begins.

"What's happening?" Gus asks.

"I don't know," Johnathan answers back.

The bright light around the airship suddenly fades and it is once again back in plain sight of the fighters. They do not hesitate.

"Launch missiles now!" Johnathan orders.

"Heat-seekers away!" Gus responds.

Gus and Johnathan watch from their cockpits as the missiles head toward the airship. Two small explosions appear at the side of the airship followed by a larger explosion on the airship's side. Next explosions occur all over the airship before the entire thing detonates in a fiery mass.

"Whoa!! Ha ha…did you see that, we got it; we got it!" Gus says excitedly.

"How? Nothing was working before."

"Well what can I tell you? I guess we hit just right," he says in a reassuring tone.

"Right okay I'll cancel the backup, let's head home," Johnathan replies.

The fighters fly off in the opposite direction.

***

Once they are gone the explosive mass suddenly shifts and disappears entirely. The airship is hidden in the clouds just above where the explosion took place, the exterior of the ship now looking like the clouds and sky. The three Americans have moved over to the observatory window as the stranger flips some switches at the wheel. With the flip of one final switch the stranger turns to the three Americans and approaches them. They look up at the still helmeted figure as he removes the helmet and acknowledges them for the first time.

"I am Captain Ryland Robur, great-great-grandson of Robur the Conqueror. Welcome aboard the Albatross."

Chapter Three
Unwanted and Unneeded

The bridge of the Albatross is deathly silent as Ryland stares at the three American soldiers who have said nothing since his introduction. Marcus's eyes have opened wide while his mouth remains slightly ajar. The colonel has taken on a stern look fixated on Ryland while keeping his military posture. An obvious look of confusion goes over Alex's face as she keeps her eyes on Ryland as well. It is Marcus who breaks the silence with a small step forward.

"Robur the Conqueror?" he asks.

"*The* Robur the Conqueror?" he asks again a little louder.

"The man who terrorized the world with death from above in the 1800s Robur the Conqueror!" he says with obvious excitement still staring directly at Ryland.

Ryland rolls his eyes.

"No, the other Robur the Conqueror who sold cookies and cakes out of his little town bakery," Ryland responds in a condescending tone before heading to one of the panels.

"Hey…" Marcus begins, watching Ryland as he walks to the panel. "Yeah okay stupid question." He finishes scratching the back of his neck.

"Robur the Conqueror? Who?" Alex asks looking toward Ryland.

"Robur the Conqueror," Colonel Winters begins not taking his eyes off Ryland, "in the late 1800s constructed a giant airship known as the Albatross when the rest of the world was still depending on hot air balloons to reach into the sky," he explains, beginning to move closer to Ryland.

"He then used it to travel the world dropping bombs on the navies and militaries of the world's countries…" he continues now stopping next to Ryland. "He claimed he was a bringer of peace…but in fact he was a murderer and a madman."

Ryland looks up from the panel he is working on meeting the colonel's gaze. Marcus and Alex go silent as the two stare each other down; an eternity seems to pass before the silence is finally broken.

"Yes…he was," Ryland answers, returning to the panel.

Alex and Marcus let out a relieved sigh as even the colonel's shoulders begin to loosen a bit though he keeps his formal stance. Ryland continues to work on the panel and ignores the colonel's presence. Unsure what to do, Alex walks over to the other side of Ryland.

"I guess you aren't following in his footsteps then?" she asks but gets no response. "Else you would have destroyed those fighters, instead of…whatever it was you   did."

"Flash Houdini," Ryland answers still keeping his eyes on the panel.

"What's that?" Marcus asks looking over the steering wheel of the Albatross.

Ryland turns to look at Marcus for a moment before returning to the panel. "A code name to activate an escape contingency plan," he answers. "The albatross is covered in small cameras and projectors which normally I use as a camouflage system, however in emergencies I use the projectors to emit a bright light.

"This temporarily blinds attacking forces. I used the distraction to hide the Albatross in the clouds. Then I used the projectors at the bottom of the ship to display an image of the Albatross off the reflection of the moisture in the air. The explosion was a recording; once the fighters thought the ship was destroyed they left. It's that simple," he finishes, a small amount of pride in his voice.

"Simple?! That's amazing!" Alex responds.

"This ship is beyond awesome!" Marcus replies coming up behind Ryland. "The department of defense doesn't have tech this advanced. I mean who designed all this stuff?"

Ryland turns from the panel and faces Marcus who is only a few feet from him. Marcus immediately straitens his posture, the slight smile on his face disappearing at Ryland's gaze.

"I did."

"Then this is not the original Albatross but a..." Colonel Winters begins.

Ryland turns to look at the colonel.

"This is the original...at least most of it," he says softening his expression. "The original was nearly destroyed, as you most likely know, by four stowaways; the ship was badly damaged but the superstructure survived and many of its systems," he explains.

Alex and Marcus look toward one another slightly uncomfortable at Ryland's last statement, however the colonel is unaffected.

"Was the wreckage left to you?" Colonel Winters presses.

"The ship was left abandoned in a secret hangar where I found it and started repairs. I upgraded the elevation technology and installed the new system you seem so impressed with..." he says, turning to Marcus before returning to the colonel.

"...after dismantling the bombs that this ship originally housed," he says rather pointedly to the colonel. All the weapons systems on my ship are non-lethal." He moves a step closer to the colonel.

"I am not my ancestor, colonel," he says in a serious tone.

Colonel Winters does not respond nor does he back away, he just keeps still, returning Ryland's unblinking gaze. Marcus and Alex fidget uncomfortably before Alex steps forward trying to break the tension.

"Well that's good..." she says coming up next to Ryland.

"Oh! We haven't been introduced!" she says with attempted enthusiasm. "My name is Alex and this is Colonel Winters." She gestures to herself and then the colonel.

"And I'm Marcus!" he cuts in extending his hand to Ryland to shake.

Ryland stares at Marcus's extended hand for a brief moment before looking up with an unwavering gaze. Marcus keeps his hand extended for a moment longer before slowly retracting it with Ryland still staring at him.

"Right...um...so thanks for saving us and everything," he says clearly uncomfortable.

"Yeah that was amazing...you really..." Alex says.

"Who were those men who attacked us?" Colonel Winters interrupts. "And that ship, you called it the Nautilus." He got Ryland's attention but no answer, just a cold stare.

"What's going on?" he presses.

"My problem and no concern of yours," Ryland finally says before proceeding out the door they entered.

"No concern of ours!" Colonel Winters says following Ryland with the other two close behind. "Our base was attacked, our soldiers slaughtered, and you say it's not our concern?" he angrily responds.

"You got it the first time, very impressive, you should be proud," Ryland sarcastically replies.

"Hey wait a minute, those freaky soldiers slaughtered our entire camp," Marcus says catching up to Ryland.

Receiving no response Alex rushes ahead of the others to get in front of Ryland, stopping him in his tracks.

"Hey!" she says with a stern expression. "It wasn't just our base that was attacked, those weird soldiers killed our friends, our brothers and if that doesn't concern us I don't know what does!" she exclaims but receives no response.

"That base was like a second home, and it was destroyed right in front of us! Now we deserve some answers!" she demands.

A moment goes by with Ryland holding Alex's gaze, all four unmoving in the corridor outside the control room. Then Ryland sighs.

"Those men are soldiers of the Nautilus," he explains. "They follow the commands of Captain Nemo."

"What!" Marcus says coming up next to Ryland. "But Captain Nemo died a hundred years ago…"

"It's not the same man!" Ryland says, clearly annoyed as he turns to Marcus.

"The original Captain Nemo died," he says in a calmer tone. "His ship was found and now a new captain is using the alias."

"Ah right," Marcus replies. "So who's the new Captain Nemo?"

"Do you not know?" Alex asks.

Ryland turns to Alex; a slight grimace comes over his face as he looks at her.

"His name is Bryant Donvain," he responds in a flat tone. "He discovered the resting place of the Nautilus a few years ago. He managed to restore it in secret and now is putting the craft to work.

"Along with a fanatically devoted crew," he finishes walking past Alex and proceeding to the staircase.

The others follow him to the Victorian staircase with Colonel Winters getting there before Alex.

"You know the man, don't you?" Colonel Winters says walking behind Ryland.

Ryland turns around to face the colonel stopping all three of them on the staircase. Ryland gives the colonel a cold stare which the colonel returns. Stopped right behind the colonel Alex sees the death glare between them and tries to break the tension.

"Why were we attacked?" she asks.

Ryland breaks the gaze with the colonel and looks back to Alex.

"I don't know," he says turning and proceeding back down the stairs. "Nemo was after something. But I won't know what until I decrypt the files from the base mainframe."

Ryland gets off the staircase two floors down from the control room with the others continuing to follow him.

"We had a surplus of weapons at the base. He must have needed—" Colonel Winters begins.

"No, he would not risk an attack like that just for supplies," Ryland says proceeding down the corridor.

"And I believe recent events have proven he has no need for your weapons. He was after something else, something that was there today," he says, suddenly halting and turning to the others.

"I don't suppose any of you know what he could have been after?"

"No, sorry," Marcus replies scratching his head.

"There was nothing new. It was just like yesterday," Alex answers.

"Clearly there was something different," Ryland presses.

"So you have no idea why we were attacked?" Colonel Winters asks.

"I know why your base was attacked, what I don't know is what he wanted."

Alex and Marcus both look confused as even the colonel's stern face breaks into a bewildered look.

"What do you mean?" Alex finally asks.

"He attacked your base because it helps his plan somehow. The question is how." Ryland turns and proceeds down the corridor again.

"What plan?" Marcus asks following Ryland with the others.

Ryland does not answer; he just proceeds down the corridor and takes a right down another hallway. Annoyed, Alex maneuvers around the others and once again gets in front of Ryland stopping him dead in his tracks.

"Please; why were we attacked? What is his plan?" she presses.

Ryland does not answer right away but stares at her with an unblinking gaze before finally letting out a deep sigh. "Captain Nemo believed my ancestor was right that the only way a peaceful world can be created is to force the world into it." He pauses for a moment before continuing.

"However, he has come to believe the human race is beyond redemption, and the only solution is to wipe the board clean. And start over," he says with a hint of shame in his voice.

"Start over..." Marcus begins. "You mean..."

Ryland breaks his gaze with Alex and turns to Marcus.

"He plans to destroy the world and then lead the few survivors to create a utopia," Ryland responds in a deadpan tone.

In another scenario this might have gotten a laugh from the three Americans, but after witnessing the destruction of their base, not to mention standing in a futuristic airship, all the trio can do is stare at Ryland with expressions of disbelief and horror.

"You can't be serious!" Colonel Winters shouts, finally breaking the silence.

"How! I mean can he actually do that?" Alex asks grabbing Ryland's arm.

"That's what I need to find out," Ryland answers turning toward Alex.

"Nemo should not be underestimated, and the Nautilus could sink an entire navy before it had torpedoes," he says ominously. "Now, there is no telling what that ship may be capable of."

"Then we need to contact the U.S. Navy and get them to track down—" the colonel begins.

"Your navy can't track the Nautilus!" he shouts turning on the colonel.

"No, the colonel is right, the navy has ways of tracking submarines," Marcus interjects.

This gets another eye roll from Ryland before he turns to Marcus.

"Your navy tracks submarines by the heat signatures from the nuclear core," Ryland responds.

"The Nautilus leaves no such trail," he says pointedly. "It runs off a cold fusion reactor with no heat trail; your navy is powerless against the Nautilus."

"Wait, you said to your computer voice thing that you could track the ship," Alex says pointing upward at the ceiling.

"I am the only one who knows how to track the Nautilus. The cold fusion reactor uses Uranium 251. This element gives off a specific radioactive signature and it's that radiation that I can track," Ryland explains.

"Uranium 251? There is no such thing," Marcus says more to himself.

"They said the same thing about this ship when it was first built. Uranium 251 is extremely rare and only occurs naturally in one place on earth. The location is known only by Nemo," Ryland explains.

"So you're tracking the Nautilus...all on your own?" Alex asks.

"He must be stopped," Ryland says. "Whatever the cost."

"On that we agree. What can we do to help?" the colonel says.

Ryland turns around to face Colonel Winters, a confused look on his face. "Help?"

"Hey this guy attacked us, we got a score to settle. So sign us up," Marcus says enthusiastically.

Colonel Winters gives Marcus a disapproving side glance before resuming his no nonsense military posture.

"In light of the circumstances we will enlist in your crew and I would like to speak to the government you answer to," Colonel Winters says in a commanding tone.

"Hey, yeah about that…where is the crew?" Alex asks looking up and down the hallway.

"There is no crew," Ryland answers.

"And I answer to no government," he replies sternly to the colonel.

"Wait, there's no crew? You're here all alone?" Alex asks.

"No government, then who do you answer to?" Colonel Winters asks.

"Myself," Ryland answers.

"But this ship…" Colonel Winters begins gesturing to the ship.

"Is privately owned."

Before Colonel Winters has a chance to respond Ryland turns to Alex. "And I installed an automated system so that I could control the Albatross without the need of a crew."

"An automated system?" Alex asks.

"The 'computer voice thing' as you put it," Ryland says gesturing air quotes. "That is the Cyber Interactive Control System and it allows one man to run a ship that once required a crew of thirty," he says with a small measure of pride in his voice.

"That's incredible! So it monitors all the systems on the ship?" Marcus excitedly asks.

"My functions include system maintenance, sensor and weapons control as well as navigation," the computerized voice suddenly answers.

All three Americans look up toward the ceiling trying to find the source of the sound while Ryland's eyes half close in slight annoyance.

"That is the Cyber Interactive Control System," Ryland explains getting the trio's attention. "It can maintain most of the ship but I am needed for the more sophisticated duties.

"Which reminds me I have systems to repair," he says again proceeding down the corridor.

"So wait, this computer system lets you run this entire airship single-handed?" Marcus asks following after Ryland with the others. "That's incredible, who designed the program?"

Ryland opens another door revealing a second Victorian spiral staircase, which he proceeds to descend with the others, close on his heels.

"I did," Ryland says still descending the stairs.

"You designed it all?" Alex asks.

"Yes," Ryland answers, a little annoyed. "I wrote and installed the initial program as well as designed and built the self-managing systems," Ryland explains with a hint of arrogance in his voice.

"That's quite impressive," Colonel Winters says following behind Ryland. "I guess I should expect nothing less from the descendent of Robur the Conqueror. He was after all a genius, albeit a deranged one."

Ryland stops at the bottom of the staircase turning to the colonel with an intense glare. Colonel Winters returns his gaze with Marcus and Alex stopped staring at the back of the colonel's head with horrified expressions on their faces.

"Yes he was," Ryland answers as he turns and enters another corridor. "Now I have work to do so the computer will lead you to the crew quarters, you can get washed up and if you so desire you can change into some of the old uniforms.

"I am afraid at present you will have to remain on the Albatross until I come to a port where I can let you off. Until then you may—" he begins to calmly explain.

"What do you mean let us off? We're staying with you!" Alex interrupts.

"The safety of the American people is at stake!" Colonel Winters follows up.

"And you can't do this alone!" Marcus interjects.

"You need us; we can—" Alex begins.

"I do not need you!" Ryland shouts. "I told you before this is none of your concern! Nemo is my problem and I will deal with him!"

"His soldiers took out our entire base in just a few minutes!" Alex counters.

"And I took them down in a few seconds! And would have stopped the Nautilus today if those fighters had not gotten in the way!" he responds obviously annoyed.

"Even if the fighters had not intervened how would you have stopped the Nautilus? I assume this ship can't sink," Marcus points out. "And from what you told us an entire navy would not be able to bring down that sub."

"A navy couldn't but I can!" Ryland shouts turning to Marcus.

"With that bomb you were talking about earlier?" Colonel Winters calmly asks.

"The Anti-Particle Bomb," Ryland answers.

"I thought you said all the weapons on your ship were non-lethal?" Marcus asks.

"They are," Ryland says calmly turning to Marcus. "That bomb is harmful only to the Nautilus itself, when it goes off it will do little damage to the structure of the ship. However it will release a form of electromagnetic radiation, which will short out the cold fusion generator on the Nautilus. The ship will be dead in the water, whatever plan Nemo has will die with the ship."

"Then let us help you!" Alex says getting in front of Ryland.

"I mean we're here anyway, we can help you," Marcus supports.

"This Nemo has declared war on the United States and it is our responsibility to stop him!" Colonel Winters says in a commanding tone.

"Enough!" Ryland shouts silencing all three of them. "Understand this Nemo is mine!" He slowly looks at all three of them.

"You have no idea what we're up against, and you'll only be in my way so the sooner I get you off my ship the better!"

"We are trained soldiers, we can—" the colonel begins to interject.

Ryland turns sharply on the colonel with more of an annoyed look than anger this time.

"Today proved that against Nemo's weapons your training means next to nothing," Ryland proclaimed. "For now I am allowing you to stay on this ship…but if you recall colonel the last time stowaways were permitted to stay on this ship it did not end well for the Albatross," he continues lowering his voice.

"So kindly let me go and see what damage was done to the bomb before I decide to learn from my ancestor and throw you off this ship!" he threatens.

"Computer!" Ryland shouts. "Lead these three to the crew quarters!"

"Right away sir," the computerized voice responds.

Lights begin to go on down the corridor from where they are standing.

"Please follow the lights and I will lead you to your destination," the voice instructs.

Ryland turns and goes down the other staircase leaving the three Americans to observe the now lit pathway they are going to take. Colonel Winters and Marcus begin to proceed down the hallway.

Alex however does not move but looks at the staircase that Ryland just descended. She calls out to the other two as they proceed down the hall. "You two go ahead, I am going to try and talk to him."

Marcus and Colonel Winters stop and turn to face her.

"I don't think that's a good idea, the guy looks pissed," Marcus replies.

"Perhaps we should give him his space," Colonel Winters agrees.

"But we need to convince him to let us help him," Alex argues looking back at the staircase. "Maybe he will feel less…threatened if just one of us talks to him."

Marcus puts his hands in his pockets and looks at the colonel who is considering the proposal.

"She could be right," Marcus says. "After all he did answer her questions. We really don't have anything to lose."

"Fine…" Colonel Winters says somewhat deterred. "Remember though," he says to Alex, "you need to convince him we all have the same enemy."

"Right," she responds nodding her head before proceeding down the staircase.

Alex goes down four floors stopping at each one to look out and see if Ryland is there; she listens for a moment figuring she will hear mechanical sounds of some kind since he went to repair the bomb. Finally when she reaches the fourth floor she hears the sounds of a wrench being cranked as she steps off the stairwell into what looks like a bomber drop port with a steampunk design to it.

In the middle of the room she sees Ryland working on a device that looks more like a satellite mixed with an iron-cast stove than a bomb and is about a foot taller than him with a jumble of wires connecting it to the roof of the room. Alex approaches Ryland cautiously; he continues to work on the device ignoring her even when she is in his line of sight.

"So…is it badly damaged?" she quietly asks.

"No," he replies never taking his eyes off the device. "The missiles just shook a few things loose. I'll have it in working order again in about half an hour."

"That's good," she responds looking over the bomb. "Is there any way I can help?"

"Do you know anything about particle radiation of elements the world does not know exists?" he asks continuing to work.

"Well…no," she responds a little uncomfortably. "But I can hand you tools or hold something."

"Not necessary."

"Right…" she says giving a half nod before stepping closer to Ryland.

"Listen I know you don't really want us here but…" she begins still clearly uncomfortable. "We have a common enemy…why shouldn't we work together?"

Ryland at last turns to Alex still kneeling in front of the open panel of the bomb.

"You are unprepared for this fight, you and your team will only get in my way," he says very calmly.

"Then prepare us!" Alex says stepping forward throwing her arms down. "Show us how to fight these people! We're fast learners! I am sure…"

"I have no time to train you," Ryland responds rising up to face her.

"Alright fine," she says stepping back a little. "Then just arm us, we will figure it out as we go."

"Arm you with my technology?" he sneers. "I don't think so." He shakes his head.

"Why?"

"Oh…that's just what your colonel wants!" he exclaims. "Him and your government, to get their hands on my tech and use it to further their political agendas!" he angrily continues.

"Well I won't have it! My ship will not be used to give one country the power to rule the world."

"My country doesn't want to rule the world!" she counters. "And if you let us contact our superiors we can make a deal and you won't have to give up any of your technology."

"And I am supposed to trust your government?" he angrily asks. "A government that would sooner kill me then Nemo."

"Not if we explain to them—" she says a little taken aback.

"Explain what?" Ryland interrupts. "Your country, like most, expects me to pay for the crimes committed by Robur the Conqueror. And you want me to put my faith in them?

"I would sooner trust a shark while holding a bleeding carcass," he angrily exclaims.

"Fine, you don't have to trust our government," she says taking a step closer to Ryland. "But let us help you. If we work together—"

"I already told you I do not need your help!" he shouts. "Now I have to focus on fixing this so please leave me alone," he says turning back to the bomb. "Just ask the computer and it will lead you to your friends. Now please go," he calmly asks.

Alex considers for a brief moment before sighing and looking upward. "Alright. Um computer…" she begins. "Can you take me to my friends?" she asks.

"Of course ma'am, this way please," the computerized voice responds.

Lights turn on behind her leading back to the spiral staircase. She begins to follow the lights before turning to take another look at Ryland.

"The colonel was right wasn't he?" she asks. "You know this Nemo…don't you?"

Ryland looks back at her from where he is working but does not answer. The two of them just hold an unwavering stare.

"We could help you get him…just think about it okay?" she requests before turning back to follow the lights.

Ryland watches her leave; for a moment his eyes dart to the side in thought before he turns back to the bomb he has been working on. He picks up a screwdriver near his feet then looks at the open panel of the bomb contemplating.

"As if they could help me," he says to himself.

Chapter Four
Caught in the Fray

A long hallway within the Albatross houses over twenty rooms of the now empty crew's quarters. The hallway is styled in the same industrial steel color that the rest of the ship is decorated with. The hallway is separated into sections divided by columns ascending to the roof of the hallway. In between the sections sliding gray doors are enclosed within large brass colored frames. Two of the doors slide open as Colonel Winters and Marcus exit different rooms wearing light grey uniforms with blue and gold cuffs, a black belt with a copper belt buckle, and an ornate bronze A on the right breast. Soon after Alex exits a third room fiddling with the same uniform.

"Not exactly fashionable," she says continuing to tug at the uniform. "Whoever made these uniforms clearly didn't take women into account." She joins Marcus and Colonel Winters in the hallway.

"Well if we're to believe these uniforms are from the original crew women were not allowed on ships back then,"

Colonel Winters states. "Even airships," he says to Alex with a light smile.

"Still, I think they're pretty cool," Marcus comments looking over the uniform. "For 1800s fashion."

Marcus makes some mock poses causing Alex to smile and Colonel Winters to shake his head in irritation.

"Right," Colonel Winters says a little louder than needed. "Alex, how went your conversation with the captain?"

"He has no intention of letting us stay any longer then he has to," she answers in a defeated tone. "And absolutely no intention of letting us, or anyone else for that matter, help him."

"Why?" Marcus asks. "I mean I know he doesn't know us but... The enemy of my enemy is my friend right?" he states looking between the two of them.

"Did you explain to him we could negotiate with our government on his behalf?" Colonel Winters asks her.

"Yes, it just upset him more," she answers. "He implied if he did our country would charge him for Robur the Conqueror's crimes.

"Actually he sounded like he knew it for a fact," she says looking directly at the colonel. "Colonel, is there a price on Ryland's head? I mean is our government holding him responsible for the crimes of Robur?" she presses the colonel.

"They can't," Marcus interjects getting both their attention. "I mean it's against the law, you can't charge the son with the crimes of the father so he can't be charged with the crimes of his great-great-grandfather, right?"

"Colonel?" she asks.

Colonel Winters looks toward both of them before responding. "I have heard of nothing concerning the arrest of Ryland Robur. Before today I assumed the Albatross had been destroyed years ago," he says taking a less formal stance. "Most don't even remember the terror from the sky, let alone the Albatross and its captain," he explains turning to Alex.

"Well, Ryland seems to think differently," she responds.

"Well regardless, we must convince him we are on his side, and to let us help him defeat this new Captain Nemo," Colonel Winters says in a commanding voice.

Marcus turns to the colonel with a surprised look on his face.

"Colonel, are you sure we should trust this man? I mean the only thing we know about him is that he controls a machine that was once used to try and conquer the world!" he argues. "And he is the descendant of the very man who tried to use this ship to conquer the world." He throws his arms down in exasperation.

Alex gives Marcus a bewildered look as she crosses her arms and takes a few steps closer to him.

"What happened to that whole 'can't judge him by the sins of his father?'" she responds clearly annoyed.

"I'm just saying he—" Marcus begins.

"Enough both of you!" Colonel Winters shouts stepping between them. "Trust or not the fact remains that our country is under attack, and this Captain Robur is the only one who seems to know how to fight them." He looks at both of them.

"Perhaps he is the only one who can stop Nemo; whatever the case we are soldiers of the United States of America and it is our responsibility to protect our nation, and it appears the way to do that is to assist the captain," he commands more than explains.

"Yeah, but you heard him, he doesn't even—" Marcus begins.

"Nautilus has been detected surfacing 100 miles directly northeast," says the computerized voice erupting through the hallway.

As soon as the trio hear the news they rush off down the hallway to the spiral staircase in order to return to the control room.

"En route to intercept the Nautilus…" the computerized voice says. "Be advised SOS signals detected from American submarine in the vicinity of the Nautilus," the computerized voice informs.

"What!?" Alex exclaims still running up the stairs.

"SOS?!" Marcus adds following behind Alex.

"He's attacking a sub!?" Colonel Winters exclaims as he exits the stairs.

With Colonel Winters in the lead the three rush down the hallway and burst into the control room. Ryland is already at the ship's wheel steering with his left hand and furiously flipping switches with his right. Alex rushes over to Ryland's side but keeps a foot away from him, Colonel Winters comes up behind her while Marcus rushes over to the observatory window.

"Ryland! What's going on?" she asks.

"The Nautilus has resurfaced," he answers still working at the controls. "I have to intercept it before it dives!"

"The computer voice said an American submarine was sending an SOS," Marcus says from the window.

"Apparently Nemo is attacking the submarine," Ryland answers unconcerned.

"Are you sure?" Colonel Winters asks.

"Nemo knows I can't track the Nautilus when he dives below 100 feet, he would not resurface without reason; we must assume he is attacking the sub," Ryland answers still steering the Albatross.

"But why attack one of our subs?" Alex asks.

"In a few minutes we can ask him," Ryland responds.

***

In the middle of the Atlantic Ocean two submarines are above water parallel to one another. On the left a modern American submarine has been forced to surface, warning sirens emanating from within with clear damage to its hull. Aquatic steampunk soldiers in diving armor are entering the American submarine through gashes in the hull. The Nautilus sits next to the heavily damaged submarine. Standing on the deck of the Nautilus, Bryant, now going by Nemo, is with a blonde-haired woman named Lt. Vernesse, both are dressed in navy blue clothes with Indian embroidered designs on the cuffs and collar.

"Most powerful navy indeed!" Lt. Vernesse sneers. "Ha! Look at them! They can't even put up a decent fight!" she says looking back to the wreck.

"We need to hurry," Nemo answers looking toward the skies. "We need to get out of here quickly!"

"But Captain, we lost the Albatross," she says turning back to face him. "There is no way Ryland can stop us!"

Before Nemo can respond the sound of roaring engines suddenly erupts through the air. Nemo and Lt. Vernesse look up to the sky in all directions before turning in the direction of the fast approaching Albatross. Nemo then looks at the stunned lieutenant.

"A lesson to be learned Lieutenant. Vernesse. One thing you must never doubt is the abilities of Ryland Robur," he exclaims looking back to the approaching Albatross.

***

Within the control room of the Albatross Ryland is still at the wheel. The Nautilus then comes into sight and Ryland's eyes and face fill with anger and a fierce determination.

"Nemo," Ryland says just barely audible to himself.

"Computer, arm the Anti-Particle Bomb and prepare for sonic barrage!" he orders moving quickly to another panel.

Colonel Winters and Alex watch him, so far just trying to stay out of his way, but years in the military have not taught the colonel to just idly stand and watch. So with a determined look of his own he approaches Ryland.

"What can we do to help?" he asks in a formal tone.

"Stay out of my way," Ryland answers side-stepping the colonel to get to another panel.

"Fire!" Ryland suddenly shouts pulling a lever at the panel.

As soon as he pulls the lever four compartments on the underside of the Albatross open up. The second they do four blue-tipped missiles launch into the water next to the Nautilus causing the entire ship to rock.

***

Nemo and his lieutenant, who have been trying to get the aquatic soldiers back into the Nautilus, are jostled but manage to stay on the deck of the Nautilus. Nemo and Vernesse recover quickly with Nemo's eyes fixated on the Albatross.

"Damn him!" Nemo curses.

Nemo then grabs a radio from his belt and speaks into it.

"Mark!" he shouts into the communicator.

"Start the ship and get us out of here!" he commands.

"We can't move sir," Mark responds over the radio. "The propellers are not responding!"

"Yet more toys Ryland," Nemo says looking back at the Albatross. "Do you get bored so easily?" he says to himself.

"Mark, are the diving ballasts still operational?" Nemo asks into the communicator.

"Yes sir, diving capability still intact," Mark responds.

"Then dive! Dive!" Nemo shouts heading toward the entrance of the Nautilus.

Small spouts of water erupt around the Nautilus as it begins to dive. Nemo and his lieutenant enter a door into the Nautilus. At the same time another explosion comes from the American submarine, black smoke pouring from the open gashes as it begins to slowly sink beneath the waves.

***

Ryland has moved back to the steering wheel while Alex and Colonel Winters have joined Marcus at the observatory window trying to get a good view of the scene below.

"Nautilus is diving. Forward propulsion in Nautilus estimated in two minutes' time," the computerized voice states.

"Computer, is the Anti-Particle Bomb ready?" Ryland asks.

"Anti-Particle Bomb still requires five more minutes to be fully charged," the automated voice answers.

Ryland rushes to another panel on the bridge as the three turn to look at him not quite sure what they should be doing.

"Damn, need to stall for time," Ryland says to himself.

"Preparing to launch Echo probe," Ryland says turning nobs at the panel.

"Launch!" he shouts looking towards the observatory window.

Another hatch at the bottom of the Albatross opens up and a small remote-control sub with a strange head resembling three speakers drops out. The machine sinks into the water and propels toward the submerging Nautilus stopping a short distance away. Once halted the device begins to send sonic pulses at the ship. The Nautilus visibly rocks from the sonic bombardment and immediately stops submerging. No sooner does this happen than Ryland rushes back to the steering wheel.

"I've got you now, nowhere to run Nemo!" Ryland excitedly shouts. "Computer, get into position and launch Anti-Particle Bomb as soon as it's ready!" he commands with a large smile on his face.

"Yes sir," the automated voice responds.

Alex and the colonel are still looking out of place as they try and figure out what they should or could be doing. Marcus however continues to look out the window as another explosion erupts from the American submarine causing both the colonel and Alex to rush to the observatory window looking down on the heavily damaged submarine. Seeing this Alex turns her attention to Ryland, who is still at the steering wheel, and rushes to his side.

"The sub…the Americans, they need help!" she tells him.

"Not important, I have Nemo at last!" he responds, eyes fixed on the Nautilus.

"Not important!" Marcus exclaims turning to look at Ryland. "Those are Americans on that sub!"

"There is nothing that can be done!" Colonel Winters remarks turning from the window.

"Can you help them?" Alex asks Ryland but gets no response.

"Can you save them?!" she yells trying to get his attention.

Alex grabs Ryland's arm finally getting him to turn to her with a fierce look on his face.

"Stopping Nemo is all that matters, I have to—" Ryland begins to explain.

"You can help them!?" Marcus exclaims walking away from the window.

Ryland looks at Marcus then back at Alex before returning his gaze to the observatory window shaking Alex off his arm in the process. Ryland is determined to ignore them and all three of them see it. The colonel's stone face is broken when he realizes this and moves directly into Ryland's line of sight.

"If you can help, then do it, save them!" Colonel Winters shouts.

"If I don't stop Nemo millions may die, I can't worry about one submarine crew!" Ryland responds trying to look past the colonel.

"One minute till Anti-Particle Bomb is fully charged," the automated voice informs the crew.

This time Alex isn't playing around as she grabs Ryland's shoulder and forces him to look right at her.

"You have to help them!" she commands.

"I have to stop Nemo!" Ryland angrily responds freeing himself from her grip.

"At any cost!? Whatever the price!? You are no different than Robur the Conqueror!" she shouts right into his face.

That last remark gets Ryland to turn to her with an angry unblinking stare still holding onto the ship's wheel. Alex stares him down with just as much determination, which Ryland does not match for long before looking back to the window. His eyes barely hit the window before he returns his gaze back to Alex then forward again. His hands clench the wheel harder; his face takes a waving grimace as his head drops a little with clenched teeth.

"Anti-Particle Bomb ready to deploy," the automated voice declares.

At the news Ryland's head jerks up and he starts furiously turning the wheel to the left. The Albatross quickly follows causing the three soldiers to lose their footing and grasp panels near them to keep upright.

"Computer!" Ryland shouts suddenly moving to another panel. "Prepare to fire all four pulse-lasers at the American submarine."

"Pulse-lasers ready, waiting for command," the automated voice answers.

All three of them look up at Ryland just managing to regain their equilibrium.

"Lasers!?" Colonel Winters asks.

"You can't destroy the submarine, those—" Marcus begins coming over to Ryland.

"Do you want me to save them!?" Ryland shouts turning to the trio. "Then get out of my way!" He returns to the panel.

The three take the hint and back away from Ryland as he turns more dials on the panel before leaving his hand hovering over a large blue button.

"Computer are we in position!?" Ryland asks.

"American submarine is directly underneath, ready to fire at your command," the automated voice answers.

"Fire!!" Ryland shouts slamming down on the button.

Four copper clad lasers emerge from beneath the ship's lower canopy. The devices light up and fire a bright white beam downwards impacting the American submarine all at once which is still sinking beneath the waves. Ryland is working furiously at another panel with the trio trying to stay out of his way. Alex moves closer to the door while Marcus and Colonel

Winters move to the window trying to see
what is happening.

"Electrical frequencies set," Ryland
says out loud. "Discharge!!"

A small green light activates on top
of all four of the copper clad lasers; arcing
electricity exits a port under the green lights
and runs down all four lasers hitting the
sinking submarine.

"Now computer, activate electric
field of the Albatross!" Ryland shouts
moving to another panel.

"Activated," the automated voice
responds.

An electric field begins to surround
the Albatross giving off a loud static sound.
Once the field surrounds the Albatross it is
then lowered slightly above the submarine.
Within in a few seconds the damaged
submarine begins to rise out of the water.
The Albatross climbs and the submarine
climbs with her until it is completely out of
the water suspended between the sea and the
Albatross in ten to fifteen feet of empty
space. On the bridge of the Albatross
warning sirens begin erupting from different
panels, the three soldiers look around the
room unclear of what they should do while
Ryland ignores the alarms altogether.

"Computer is the submarine out of
the water!?" Ryland asks.

"Submarine is fully out of the water," the automated voice answers.

"Out of the water!" Alex exclaims looking toward Ryland.

"That's…but…that's not possible! How are…" Marcus says looking out the window.

More alarms begin to go off around the control room as a groaning sound begins to emit from the hull. Marcus, Alex, and Colonel Winters all look around at the different panels going off before rushing over to Ryland who is still furiously working at a control panel ignoring the alarms.

"Computer, connect with the Echo Probe and prepare to transmit instructions immediately!" Ryland commands.

"Echo Probe ready to receive instructions," the automated voice responds.

"What are you doing!?" Alex shouts over the alarms.

"Almost done," Ryland says clearly ignoring her.

"Done with what?" Alex probes to no avail.

"Nautilus has regained forward propulsion and is fleeing, do you wish to pursue, Captain?" the automated voice asks.

Ryland looks up from the panel with the warning sirens and sounds of straining metal still present. He looks down at Alex at his side and an annoyed look flashes across his face before he continues to type at the panel.

"No! Stay here, computer track the Nautilus for as long as possible!" Ryland answers clearly conflicted. "Now, open transmission to the echo probe."

"Probe ready to receive program," the automated voice answers.

"Transmit now!" Ryland shouts.

The remote-control sub, known as the Echo Probe, lights up and rushes forward beneath the levitating submarine. Once beneath the sub, sonic pulses emit from the device sending frequencies that slow down the vibrations of the water molecules. The water around the probe begins to turn to a thick layer of ice. The Echo Probe begins to swirl moving slowly beneath the submarine as the water gradually turns to a large layer of ice bigger than the submarine suspended above the water. Ryland enters a final code into the panel before rushing past the trio and back to the steering wheel. Marcus and Alex are still attempting to stay out of his way but Colonel Winters marches right over to Ryland.

"You have to stop this!" he exclaims. "Whatever you're trying to do its tearing your ship apart!" Colonel Winters shouts trying to get a response.

"The ship does not need to hold forever," Ryland answers not looking at the colonel. "Just till the probe has—"

"The Echo Probe has completed its task," the automated voice interrupts.

"Computer get ready to release the submarine on my mark!" Ryland commands.

The Albatross descends slowly, the submarine descending with it until the sub rests on the large layer of ice, a wave splashing out as it comes to rest. Once settled on the ice the arcing electricity from the pulse lasers shuts off. The field around the Albatross soon dissipates before the ship begins to climb away from the American submarine now resting on the ice. Aboard the now ascending Albatross Marcus is staring out the window with Alex at his side; the colonel has not moved from Ryland's side. Once the submarine rests on the ice Marcus and Alex excitedly turn to Ryland and the colonel.

"You did it!" Marcus and Alex exclaim in unison.

"You really did it, you saved the sub!" Alex remarks rushing over to Ryland.

"That was amaz—" Marcus begins to say coming over to Ryland.

Before either of them can get to Ryland, he rushes past them to a panel at the far end of the bridge.

"Computer where is the Nautilus!" Ryland shouts staring at the screen on the panel.

A moment goes by with Ryland staring at a static filled screen and receiving no answer from the computerized voice.

"Computer!!" Ryland impatiently shouts.

"Nautilus has dived beneath the sea, I am unable to track its movements further," the automated voice answers.

"Well, where was it headed, in what direction!?" he angrily demands looking up toward the ceiling.

"Electromagnetic fields disrupted my sensors, I have no way of determining what direction the Nautilus took," the voice explains.

"Damn!!" Ryland says slamming his fists against the nearest panel. "I've lost him; he's gotten away from me again!" he shouts, fists still clutched on the panel.

Marcus and Colonel Winters exchange troubled looks while Alex moves towards Ryland and puts her hand on his shoulder.

"I'm sorry, it wasn't your fault," she says in a soothing voice.

"I'm aware of that!" Ryland responds turning sharply on her.

Ryland's eyes rise and shrink with hatred as he stares Alex down causing her to back away from him. Colonel Winters and Marcus both step forward toward Alex.

"And what do you mean by that?" Colonel Winters asks.

"It's your fault he got away!" Ryland responds looking at all three of them. "I had him in my grasp and you—"

"What?" Marcus interrupts stepping in front of Ryland. "Made you save an entire crew who were about to die!" he fires back.

"You saved those men, they're still alive because of you!" Alex exclaims gesturing to the observatory window.

"No! Because of you!" Ryland answers pointing to Alex. "And because of you Nemo is gone and I have no idea where!"

"Calm down, we'll help you find him again!" Colonel Winters intervenes.

"How? You are not part of this!" Ryland shouts at the colonel. "You are dead weight!" He steps up to the colonel. "Dead weight that I should have gotten rid of from the start!" he says looking at all three of them.

"But you're right it is not my fault Nemo got away...it's yours," he says pointing at them. "And anyone who dies from this point on is on your heads!" He angrily walks off the bridge.

Alex is about to follow him but the colonel grabs her shoulder stopping her short. She turns her head to protest but the colonel just shakes his head indicating her to stay. She looks over to Marcus who just shakes his head in response knowing she is defeated. Alex stays put and simply looks back at the door Ryland exited from.

Chapter Five
Storm's Eye

Beneath the waves of the Atlantic Ocean the Nautilus cuts through the waters at a speed that makes even the most modern submarine look like a tugboat. Within the antique ship, through the beautiful salon that the ship boasted, lies a bronze colored door covered with an ornate N surrounded with Indian designs—the captain's quarters, where Nemo sits behind a lavish mahogany desk covered with charts, a few books, and writing utensils. He is in a simple office chair, deep in thought, ignoring the crewman right in front of him. Lt. Vernesse is standing at his side looking between the speaking crewman and Nemo.

"Fine!" Nemo says interrupting the crewman. "Now back to your post and inform me when we reach our next destination." Nemo stands from his chair.

"Yes sir!" the crewmember answers before turning to leave.

"Why do you look so troubled?" Lt. Vernesse asks coming over to Nemo's side.

"We got what we needed and got away from Ryland scratch free."

"That is exactly what is troubling me," Nemo responds turning to her.

"That we got away?"

"Yes," Nemo exclaims moving to the other side of his desk.

"He had us...we were in his hands, and he lets us go." He picks up a book on his desk. "To save the lives of the men on that sub?" he asks in a confused tone.

"Well he is trying to stop us from destroying the world," she answers walking over to the opposite side of his desk.

"Ryland does not give a damn about the world! And he cares even less about people's lives," Nemo explains looking back to his desk. "He wouldn't stop to help someone if his own life depended on it. So what changed?"

"You think he suddenly gained a sense of empathy or something?" she wonders.

"I don't know. But something is going on, something has happened to my old friend. For some reason he has decided to care about others." He crosses his arms behind his back.

"Isn't that a good thing?" she asks approaching him. "If he is no longer willing to do whatever is necessary then doesn't that create a weakness we can exploit?"

"A Ryland Robur who cares about others, that's something I could never imagine of my dear old friend," he states more to himself than the lieutenant. "It could make him vulnerable.

"Or it could make him a greater threat than ever," Nemo exclaims.

***

On board the Albatross Ryland is uncertain of his next move, unsure of how to proceed with his self-appointed mission. It's not the first time, whenever he got stuck he would do what he did best, he would build or repair something. This time was no different, after his outburst at the three soldiers he had proceeded down the spiral staircase and gotten off four floors down. From there he proceeded down another hallway and opened a door that had its original label scraped off. When the ship belonged to Robur the Conqueror this room had served as the armory housing guns, explosives, and volatile chemicals that had been used in Robur's bombs.

Now that Ryland had renovated the ship the armory was an experimental laboratory resembling more of a Victorian style mechanic's garage. The walls were still the original industrial steel color with holes strewn about where weapons racks used to be placed. Now however the walls were covered with desks and tool chests, pieces of different machines on the tables. One machine, which looks like a bronze version of Sputnik with a Tesla coil protruding from it, has Ryland's undivided attention.

It took Alex awhile to convince the others to let her go and talk to Ryland but after some arguing they agreed that Ryland seemed less hostile around her. Finding where Ryland was on the ship was actually easy once Marcus had the bright idea to ask the ship. The automated system was happy to oblige and guided Alex right to the door of the lab.

She enters with the door opening rather loudly, however Ryland doesn't look up and simply continues using a screwdriver to work on the Sputnik-like device. Alex enters and stands a few feet to the side of him before fidgeting uncomfortably trying to come up with something to say.

"So…anyway," she finally begins. "Do you need any…? Oh right, no you don't," she says looking over the strange device.

"Thank you, Alexandria," Ryland suddenly says looking up from the device.

Of all the things that Alex had mentally prepared for that Ryland would say to her that was definitely not one of them. It surprised her so much that for a moment she just stared at him blankly while he stared back.

"For what?" she asks finally regaining her senses.

"You were right," he states. "I did need to save those men, I can't prove that I am better than my ancestor if I act just like him," he explains with a sincere look on his face. "So thank you Alexandria." He puts the screwdriver down on the table.

"It's just Alex," she responds with a slight smile. "And for what it's worth, I don't think you're anything like your ancestor." She steps to the other side of the table.

"Only time will tell Alexandria," he replies with a slight smirk. "In the meantime I apologize for earlier, it was wrong to blame you for Nemo getting away."

"Is there really no way to track him, or figure out where he is going to strike next?" she asks moving around the table.

"No," Ryland answers lightly shaking his head. "Once the Nautilus dives she's invisible," he explains turning toward her. "I have to wait for her to resurface, and even then…" He pauses.

"The range on my ship, albeit impressive, is still limited," he states looking around the room.

"So…there's really nothing we can do?" she inquires.

"Sit tight and hope we are in range when the Nautilus resurfaces," Ryland answers as he leans on the table with his arms folded, a slight look of defeat on his face. "Nothing else we can do."

Neither of them speaks for a few seconds, Ryland just leans against the table looking downwards with that same defeated look. Alex is trying to think of something comforting to say but what comes to mind does not seem like it would be comforting to someone like Ryland, until an idea pops into her head.

"Was there nothing in those computer files that might give us a clue?" she asks.

Ryland looks up at her with a puzzled expression on his face. "Computer files?"

"The ones you took from our base," she explains. "You said you were decry—"

Before she can finish her sentence, Ryland springs up from the table excitedly grabbing her shoulders. "You're right! How could I have forgotten?"

"Computer!" he calls out letting go of Alex. "Have you finished decrypting the files from the army base?"

"Files fully decrypted and awaiting review," the automated voice replies.

Before the computerized voice even finishes the statement he rushes out of the lab with Alex quickly following him.

"We might not be out of this yet!" he excitedly calls back to Alex.

"Hey wait!!" Alex calls hot on Ryland's heels.

Colonel Winters and Marcus are still on the bridge looking over the various panels and controls while being very careful not to actually touch anything. Both of them back off from the panels as Ryland bursts into the control room and immediately starts working at one of the control panels. Alex follows shortly afterwards and stops next to Ryland. After the initial shock of Ryland's sudden entrance wears off Marcus and the colonel proceed to join Alex and Ryland.

"Alex what's going on?" Colonel Winters asks.

"He's looking through the files he took from our base, we think there might be a clue to catch the Nautilus," she replies.

"Great!" Marcus excitedly says. "Did you find anything Ryland?"

"Mostly nonsense," Ryland answers looking at the screen. "Supplies, rations, arrivals, personnel, nothing that's going to point the way to—"

"Wait!" Colonel Winters interrupts, stepping next to Ryland. "Go back up, back to the personnel on the base," he says pointing at the screen.

Ryland looks at the colonel curiously for a moment before returning his gaze to the screen and obliging. "What is it?"

"Right here." Colonel Winters points to the screen. "General Matthews. I served with him a couple of years ago. I never knew he was at the base, and I saw almost everyone there."

"Really?" Ryland asks looking back to the screen. "A general at the base on the same day Nemo attacks."

"Hell of a coincidence if you ask me," Marcus responds.

"You think it was the general Nemo was after?" Colonel Winters ask Ryland.

"Let's find out shall we?" Ryland answers beginning to type at the panel.

"General Matthews arrived the day of the attack," he says reading from the screen. "According to this he was having some information destroyed."

"What information?" Marcus asks.

"There's no record," Ryland answers searching through the files. "Whatever it was it wasn't entered into the database."

"Well maybe the documents were destroyed before Nemo could get his hands on them," Alex responds hopefully.

"Perhaps," Ryland says with his hands moving to a thinking position. "But if that were the case why would Nemo attack the submarine? It seems more likely he was proceeding to next step."

"Anyway Nemo was always lucky, it would be best to assume he got the information he wanted," a touch of annoyance coming out in the last words.

"So we're back to square one?" Marcus says a little disappointed.

"Not necessarily," Ryland answers again typing at the panel. "We have the general's bio, if we look at everything he's done over his career we might be able to figure out what Nemo wanted."

The screen lights up and a bio with the general's picture comes up. Ryland begins reading.

"Mostly information gathering and training," Ryland says reading the screen. "He was active in the Cold War, but nothing really jumps out, certainly nothing that Nemo could use to destroy the world.

"Wait," he says suddenly stopping the screen.

"What is it?" Alex asks getting a closer look at the screen.

"Did you find something?" the colonel asks.

"The general worked in strategic air-strikes during the Cold War," Ryland reads off the screen. "I wonder…maybe; computer, has the American submarine been rescued yet?"

"Reports say all hands have been rescued and officials are assessing the damage to the submarine before the ice melts," the automated voice answers.

"What have they found?" Ryland asks looking upwards.

"Signal is encrypted several hours will be required before reports can be seen," the automated voice answers.

"Damn! Alright, decrypt the files as—" Ryland begins.

"Hours!" Marcus interrupts.

"Ha! Here let me," Marcus says suddenly shoving Ryland out of the way to type at the panel.

"What?" Ryland asks.

"Please, I've been hacking into encrypted signals for ages," Marcus replies furiously typing.

"You mean you can get the reports?" Ryland asks. "How soon?"

"Just about…" he replies still typing.

"Now!" He says triumphantly.

Marcus turns around with a huge grin plastered on his face to look at Ryland who is just staring at the computer screen in total disbelief, something that obviously does not happen often to him. He quickly recovers.

"Well done," Ryland compliments.

"Alright Marcus!" Alex exclaims patting Marcus on the back.

"Well done," Colonel Winters responds standing up straight with his arms crossed behind his back. "And exactly how long have you been hacking into secured military signals?" he asks with a rather stern look on his face.

"Well," Marcus replies with a very guilty look on his face, "you know, it was more of a hobby, just something I did—"

"That's it!" Ryland suddenly interrupts. "That's his game!" he states turning to the three of them.

"What is?" Alex asks.

"You figured it out?" Marcus adds.

"The report shows that the submarine was carrying nuclear missiles when it was attacked," Ryland reads off the screen. "And the Nautilus seems to have hit the submarine close enough to get to the missiles without damaging them."

"You mean he stole the submarine's nuclear missiles!!" Colonel Winters exclaims looking at the screen.

"No," Ryland answers looking toward the colonel. "Not the missiles; the plutonium, the nuclear material!" he says with a pleased look on his face.

"He stole the nuclear material but not the missiles themselves?" Alex asks.

"Because the missiles are encrypted!" Marcus excitedly exclaims.

"Nemo can't fire the missiles without codes from the Whitehouse!" Marcus explains.

"So he removed the dangerous material instead?" Alex asks still confused.

"Exactly!!" Ryland answers.

"Wait! So he has the radioactive material?" Colonel Winters inquires. "But how is he going to use it? Is he going to transplant dirty bombs over the world?"

"No Colonel, that's where our general comes into this," Ryland replies pointing to the screen. "According to his records he worked in strategic air-strike defenses.

"Now," he begins turning back to the colonel, "during the Cold War your government hid missiles and silos all over the country in preparation for a nuclear war, but since the fall of the Soviet Union most have been decommissioned."

"So he wants to use the missiles that haven't been disarmed yet?!" Alex interrupts.

"No," Ryland answers. "Those missiles are still encrypted and guarded, what he wants is the missiles that have had their radioactive material removed, and had their encrypted code disabled!" he explains, a light smirk on his face.

"He's taking the empty shells and arming them with the plutonium he stole from the sub!" Marcus exclaims.

"Then he reactivates the missiles and launches them at our enemies!" Alex responds.

"Starting a nuclear world war!" Colonel Winters says calmly.

"And decimating the world as you know it," Ryland says.

"With Nemo safe under the sea he can wait out the worst of it and rise up to lead the survivors when it's finished," Ryland explains shaking his head.

"We have to do something!" Marcus exclaims. "Call our superiors! The army—" he suggests.

"And tell them what?" Ryland interrupts. "The descendent of Robur the Conqueror has uncovered a plot by Captain Nemo to start a third world war," he sarcastically states.

"Yeah, I'd love to see how that conversation goes," he says rolling his eyes.

"Well we have to do something!" Alex interjects.

"We can't just—" Colonel Winters begins.

"I am not just going to stand here," Ryland interrupts standing in front of the colonel. "I am going after him, I just have to figure out exactly where he's going," Ryland says walking over to a panel.

"What do you mean?" Alex asks coming over to the panel.

"There were several silos peppered all over your country," he says typing at the panel. "However, Nemo needs to arm the missiles and launch them before I can stop him, so he won't go around arming missiles and then waiting to launch them, he will go after one large collection clustered in one area, arm all the decommissioned missiles and launch them all at once."

"But how will we know exactly which one he's going to choose?" Colonel Winters asks.

"Easy, we just need to hack into the pentagon's archives and then…" he begins.

"What?" he says looking at the screen.

"No! They've changed their firewalls…" he explains clearly annoyed. "…sooner than I expected, it's going to take me time to…" He stops, looking over at Marcus.

"Unless?" Ryland asks tilting his head at the panel.

Marcus responds with a wide grin, flexing his fingers before he steps to the panel.

"Easy," he confidently remarks taking Ryland's position at the panel. "Especially with your systems." He begins to type.

The others gather round Marcus as he furiously types at the keyboard, the screen flashes different systems of code and military firewalls of the Pentagon. With the advanced systems on the Albatross, as well as the help of the automated system, Marcus is able to break through the firewalls in just fifteen minutes, to the congratulations of Ryland and Alex and the slight disapproval of Colonel Winters.

"Okay, I'm in, now what am I looking for?" Marcus says.

"Missile silo locations, and look for recently disarmed ones," Ryland answers looking over Marcus's shoulder.

Marcus returns his attention to the screen once again typing away; within a few minutes the screen displays a large map of the United States of America. On the map are scattered red dots showing the still active missile silos mixed with scattered blue dots showing the decommissioned silos. Small dates can be seen next to each light and as the four look over the map they notice two large clusters of blue lights: the first in North Carolina, and the second in South Dakota.

"It's going to be one of these two," Ryland says pointing to the screen.

"But which one?" Alex asks looking at Ryland.

"Probably this one," Colonel Winters suggests pointing to the cluster in North Carolina. "It's closest to the sea, and the Nautilus is a submarine."

"Great, then let's get going!" Marcus exclaims turning from the panel.

"No!" Ryland interjects. "That's not where he's heading, he's going for the cluster in South Dakota." He heads to the wheel.

"What do you mean?" Colonel Winters asks following Ryland with the others. "North Carolina is closer to the sea."

"Exactly!" Ryland answers turning to all three of them. "Nemo is not stupid and he knows me; he would make contingencies for the event I figured out his plans, no matter how unlikely."

"So you think that North Carolina is too obvious and therefore he'll choose the other location?" Marcus asks.

"Without a doubt, he's heading for South Dakota." Ryland agrees.

"You can't be sure of that," Colonel Winters interjects. "If we head off in the wrong direction we could miss him entirely."

"True," Ryland answers setting controls next to the wheel. "But South Dakota makes sense for other reasons too. Most of the old silos were on the eastern coast for shorter distance," he says pointing to the screen. "The other countries knew this and are monitoring the sky from the east to this day."

"However in South Dakota the missiles will have to be fired from the west," Ryland points out.

"So the other countries' defenses won't pick them up as fast," Alex exclaims.

"And when they do it will be too late," Marcus adds.

"It makes sense, colonel," she says reassuringly.

Colonel Winters looks at both his soldiers before resuming his military position and walking to Ryland. He stops less than a foot from Ryland, having to look up at the six foot three Ryland.

"Are you sure about this?" Colonel Winters asks.

"I'm sure," Ryland answers without hesitation.

"Then you had better show us how fast this hot air balloon can really go," he says.

"You asked for it," Ryland answers with a smirk.

Ryland turns back to the controls next to the steering wheel and manipulates a few buttons and knobs before pulling a lever, launching the Albatross forward. The three soldiers stumble a bit but quickly regain their footing as Ryland sets a few more controls around the wheel.

"Computer, engage auto pilot, inform me when we are near the destination, and scan for the electromagnetic fields of the guns...and tell me as soon as you scan them!" Ryland commands.

"Understood, scanners now calibrated to scan for Nautilus firearms," the automated voice responds.

"Right, so what's the plan?" Alex asks stepping next to Ryland.

"Plan?" Ryland asks with a confused look on his face.

"You can't just go after Nemo, we need a plan of attack," Colonel Winters states in a commanding voice.

"Yeah, we can't just rush into a fight," Marcus adds.

"I have a plan...but why should that concern you three?" Ryland asks looking at the three of them.

"Why should it concern us?" Colonel Winters says with a tone of disbelief.

"You are joking?" Alex asks exasperated.

"I told you before this does not concern you, Nemo is my responsibility and I will stop him." Ryland responds.

"But we helped you!" Marcus interjects.

"You wouldn't have any idea what Nemo was up to if it wasn't for us!" Colonel Winters shouts.

"Yes, and I am grateful to you, truly I am," Ryland says calmly. "But that does not change the fact that you three are unequipped to fight Nemo." Ryland turns to exit the bridge.

"Then equip us!" Alex says grabbing his arm. "It's going to take some time to get to South Dakota."

"And it's obvious you do not intend to drop us off just yet," Colonel Winters interjects.

"So you might as well let us help," Marcus says.

"This is not up for debate!" Ryland shouts. "You three are at best stowaways! I did not ask for you to come here and I do not need your help!"

"Fine you don't need us, but Nemo is trying to destroy our country not yours, if this concerns anyone it's us!!" Alex shouts pointing to herself and the others. "So help us defend our homes!"

"Please Ryland we need you to help us," she says calmly stepping up to Ryland.

A moment goes by where Ryland and Alex stare each other down before Ryland looks up and scans the other two soldiers who are also standing steadfast with determined looks on their faces. Ryland looks back to Alex whose gaze has not wavered; another moment passes before he takes a deep breath.

"Follow me," Ryland says turning to exit the bridge.

All three of them quickly follow as Ryland takes them down the hallway and begins to proceed down the spiral staircase talking all the way.

"Nemo's soldiers use guns that fire a device called a Leyden bullet," he explains. "This bullet contains a lethal charge of electricity. If it hits you, even with a bulletproof vest the discharging electricity will kill you, that's how your friends at the military base were taken out so quickly.

"Now the guns do have a weakness; if a directional electromagnetic field is aimed at the guns, it will overwhelm the bullets and cause them to discharge inside the barrels," he explains stepping off the staircase into a hallway.

"That's that dish weapon you used right?" Marcus chimes in.

"Electro-Amplifier; correct," Ryland answers as he turns to one of the doors and enters it. "Unfortunately I only have one of them," he explains as the others enter the room.

The room is decorated in the same color as the other rooms, this one filled with shelves and black cabinets with silver handles.

"But one shot can take out several of those guns in range. However, even without their guns Nemo's men are well trained, and skilled at hand to hand combat," Ryland says as he walks over to one of the cabinets. "So I am going to arm you with these Electro-Sonic bolts," he says opening the cabinet door.

"What are those?" Alex and Marcus say in unison.

"A non-lethal weapon that arcs high voltage electricity," Ryland explains pulling out the steampunk styled single stick he wielded earlier. "One touch can knock out your opponent for a couple of hours."

"So it's a stun baton?" Colonel Winters asks looking at the device.

"In a sense," Ryland answers a bit annoyed. "But this weapon also uses high sonic frequencies to disrupt the air, creating a channel so the electricity can be fired at a nearby soldier."

"So it shoots electricity! That is way cool!" Marcus excitedly says.

"Yes," Ryland says handing one of the Sonic-Bolts to Marcus.

"Now you have to watch the power levels of the weapon," Ryland explains grabbing another Sonic-Bolt. "How much energy it has is displayed on a small bar on the side. If it is running low, take the strap at the end and spin it like so," he instructs, spinning the weapon vertical to his body.

"The kinetic energy will recharge the device, understand?" he asks looking to the three of them.

They nod in agreement, and Ryland stops spinning the weapon, handing it to Alex and then proceeding to retrieve one each for Colonel Winters and himself.

"This switch to turn it on?" Alex asks looking over the Sonic-Bolt.

"Right. To fire electricity twist the top and hit the same button," he explains with his Sonic-Bolt.

"What's the range on these things?" Marcus asks looking over his device.

"Depending on the power…10 to 15 feet," Ryland answers.

"Is this all you have?" Colonel Winters asks looking over the Sonic-Bolt.

"I told you, colonel, I got rid of the weapons my ancestor used," Ryland answers. "Besides, this is not all we have, we also have the Albatross. And the ship is linked with my phone so I can use its defenses without being on the bridge." He pulls out his phone.

Ryland opens another drawer and takes out the strange dish weapon from before. He checks it then collapses it. He walks over to another cabinet and grabs a satchel bag which he slings over his shoulder before placing his weapons inside it. He turns back to the three of them who are still examining the Sonic-Bolts.

"That reminds me," he says snapping his fingers.

Ryland moves over to another drawer, opening it and taking out three silver-colored ornately designed bracelets. Ryland hands each one of them a bracelet which they take with a confused look on their faces.

"These serve the multiple purpose of identifying you to the Albatross, protecting you from its defenses, and absorbing some of the current if you're hit with a Leyden Bullet," Ryland explains.

"Now while this will keep you from being killed by them, you could still be knocked unconscious for several hours, and if you get hit by more than one at once...well...don't," he says calmly.

"By the way Marcus," he says reaching into his satchel, "you should be able to use this." Ryland gives Marcus a large bronze-colored cylinder flash drive.

"What is it?" Marcus asks taking the device.

"It's a code breaker, it can tear through most firewalls in seconds. Since you're insisting on accompanying me, you might as well be useful," he says sarcastically.

"Now with my luck Nemo's soldiers will have already started arming the missiles," he says with an annoyed tone in his voice. "We are going to have to go in and try to delay them long enough for you, Marcus, to get into the system control of the missiles and permanently disarm them. And if we are very fortunate we just might get Nemo in the process," he states though not particularly hopeful.

"We definitely will!" Alex exclaims patting Ryland on the shoulder.

"Or we will die trying," Colonel Winters states holding up his Sonic-Bolt.

"Hey no worries colonel, you heard Ryland, while we're wearing these," Marcus says pointing to his bracelet, "Nemo's soldiers can't kill us, right Ryland?"

"Right." Ryland nods. "Theoretically," he adds.

"Theoretically?" Marcus asks.

"Wait, that's what you said," Marcus states a little worried.

"Yes that is what they do but…" Ryland begins, looking a little sheepish.

"But?" all three of them ask.

"But…they…really have never been tested," he responds.

"Never!" Marcus exclaims.

"Don't worry, I'm...decently sure they will work," Ryland replies though not very assuredly.

"Decently sure?!" Alex inquires.

"Approaching destination, Nemo's soldiers have been detected, arrival in five minutes," the automated voice suddenly interrupts.

The four of them look up to the ceiling before Ryland, followed closely by the others, rushes out of the room and heads towards the staircase. This time however Ryland heads down the staircase instead of up, throwing the soldiers, but they soon recover and proceed to follow him. He exits the staircase into the departure bay of the Albatross, the same room the three soldiers had rushed into when their base was attacked. Ryland does not head to the door but instead goes to the far left of the room where a large circular structure is protruding from the floor. The three of them follow him as he begins to push controls on a panel next to the structure.

"Computer how many soldiers do you detect?" Ryland asks.

"Sensors detect fifteen electromagnetic signatures. I am also picking up readings of specialized equipment coming from the silos," the computerized voice responds.

"They can't already be in there!" Marcus exclaims in disbelief.

"Don't those silos have alarms or something?" Alex asks with the same tone of disbelief.

"They must have disabled the alarms," Colonel Winters states. "That's the only way Nemo could convince the world America started a world war," he says to Ryland.

"Correct and if we don't hurry, that's exactly what's going to happen!" Ryland replies. "Computer, engage camouflage," he orders.

"Hope you three are ready, if you lose this fight, you lose everything," he says looking to the circular structure in front of him.

Chapter Six
Storm Front

Before anything further can be said Ryland turns a dial on the panel and the large cylinder structure opens revealing the surface below. As the floor doors open up four bronze-colored handgrips connected to black cables descend from the ceiling. Without a word Ryland grabs one of the handles and jumps down through the opening. The others watch in horror before quickly looking over the side of the opening to see Ryland slowly descending to the ground. The three soldiers look up at the remaining cables before turning to look at one another.

After a moment of silence Marcus shrugs and grabs the cable closest to him. With a final look at the others and a deep breath he jumps through the opening. Alex and Colonel Winters are quick to follow as they join Marcus on a grassy hill below. Ryland is not far off heading for a large rectangular cement structure. The top of this structure bears a large steel trapdoor which has been clearly twisted open.

The others catch up to Ryland just as he reaches the concrete structure. Colonel Winters takes the lead and cautiously approaches the wrenched-open door. He takes out his Sonic-Bolt and aims it down the trapdoor with Ryland watching a bit perplexed at the whole display. Once Colonel Winters has scanned the entrance he makes a quick gesture with his left hand. Marcus and Alex respond immediately and come up to next to Colonel Winters as he begins to proceed down the stairs. For a moment Ryland just confusedly stares at the strange display before following them.

They proceed down the trapdoor into a long concrete hallway before coming to a large underground hangar. Pipes, electrical cables, and other various cables are scattered around the area with the tops of eight large missiles clearly visible. Scattered around the room are also a number of soldiers from the Nautilus working on the missiles. Toward the left-hand corner of the hangar sits a control room on large steel beams; two other soldiers can be seen through the windows of the control room.

Colonel Winters and the other Americans are tight against the concrete wall taking short glances at the scene. Ryland is right behind them still watching their movements in slight confusion.

Colonel Winters then spots some large containers. He makes another gesture and all three rush to hide behind the containers. Ryland soon joins them.

"Well, so far so good," Marcus whispers to Ryland. "You think they would have put some guards at the entrance or something."

"I said Nemo's men were fanatically loyal, I never said they were bright," Ryland whispers back.

"We're badly outnumbered," Alex whispers looking from behind the containers. "What's our next move?" she asks turning to Ryland.

"They're farther along than I anticipated," Ryland responds scanning the scene. "If we attack, those men in the control room might launch some of the missiles."

"So what do you propose?" Colonel Winters asks.

"I could use the Albatross to fire sonic pulses at the control room, and give Marcus a chance to get there and disable the controls, but..." Ryland answers.

"But?" Alex asks.

"If I use that on this base I will trip the secondary alarms, and your government will respond," Ryland explains.

"Isn't that a good thing?" Marcus asks. "I mean by the looks of things we need all the help we can get."

"There is no telling how they will respond," Ryland answers looking directly at Marcus. "They may send fighters or a survey team, either way more trouble than help, and if they send fighters at close range they will be able to detect the Albatross."

"We are wasting time," Colonel Winters interrupts still whispering. "We need to stop this now, so decide whatever you want, but do it now!"

Ryland looks at the others before taking out his cell phone and clicking a few buttons.

"Computer, sonic barrage 100 feet north-west of my current position," Ryland whispers into the phone.

Ryland puts away his phone and then pulls the dish weapon out of his satchel.

"Get ready," he says turning to the others. "As soon as the pulses hit go after the soldiers. Marcus, you get to that control room and try to disable the launching mechanism."

Marcus nods in response as he, Colonel Winters, and Alex prepare their Sonic-Bolts. They then move unseen into the hangar, ducking behind various materials from the 1960s now deactivated. Suddenly a shrieking noise is heard as the entire base is physically rocked by the concussive force of the Albatross, electrical components are shaken loose and soldiers are knocked about like rag dolls. Ryland and the others move through the chaos trying not to draw attention to themselves until absolutely necessary. The shrieking gets louder as they come into range of the soldiers. Marcus moves ahead and the others pause as the shrieking comes to an end, and before the soldiers can fully recover Ryland stands and fires his dish weapon. The soldiers' guns immediately spark and arc electricity forcing them to throw them down.

In a swift, and clearly over-practiced move, Ryland slips his dish weapon back into his bag and pulls out his Electro-Sonic Bolt.

"Take them!!!" he shouts.

Alex and Colonel Winters rush toward the still disoriented soldiers with their Electro-Sonic Bolts as Ryland remains in place firing electric arcs from his.

Marcus is rushing toward the missile control room while Ryland and the others take on Nemo's soldiers. Staying low and keeping out of sight Marcus manages to ascend the stairs to the control room without being seen. Inside two of Nemo's technicians, Caleb and David, who are dressed in simple navy blue and silver uniforms without armor, are just beginning to recover from the concussive blasts of the Albatross.

"Oh, my head! What happened?" Caleb says slowly getting to his feet.

"Some kind of earthquake?" David groggily responds rubbing his head.

"In South Dakota?" Caleb asks, supporting his weight on one of the nearby computers.

"Well maybe..." David begins getting to his feet.

"What the...?" he exclaims looking out the window.

"What?" Caleb asks looking out the window as well.

"We're under attack!" David exclaims, pointing.

Before Caleb or David can react any further, Marcus bursts in through the door letting the sound of the electric firefight outside into the soundproof room. Marcus aims his weapon and with a burst of electricity quickly knocks out both technicians. Marcus scans them quickly to see they are unconscious before running to the nearest panel. Once there he inserts the adaptable end of the flash drive device into the 1960s computer silently praying that it can properly interface with the ancient computer system. To his obvious relief the drive works perfectly giving him access. Marcus goes to work furiously typing away to diffuse the systems.

Outside Ryland, Alex, and Colonel Winters have all engaged in close-quarters combat with the aquatic soldiers; although disarmed they prove to be competent fighters. Alex and Colonel Winters are obviously unfamiliar with the bizarre Indian style of the soldiers attacks as their jumping and twirls make it look more like a dance then a fight. Ryland proves more experienced as he matches them with a similar, yet less flashy, fighting style and manages to take out more soldiers. Before they can disable all the men around them more aquatic soldiers whose guns still work come to join the fight.

Alex spots them and the three of them duck for cover to begin using the long-range feature on their weapons to keep them at bay. The aquatic soldiers take cover in turn and an electrical firefight ensues as the enemies' electric bullets spark on collision with the containers they are hiding behind. In turn the arcing electricity electrocutes the cover of the aquatic soldiers. There are far more of the soldiers and they are only managing to keep them at bay when

Ryland's phone begins to let out a loud warning signal. Without a word he stops firing and pulls out his phone.

"What?" he asks speaking into the phone.

"American fighters have been dispatched. Albatross will soon be in radar range," the automated voice responds loud enough for only Ryland to hear.

"Oh perfect!" he exclaims putting away his phone.

"What is it?" Alex asks ducking back down after firing her weapon.

"Your government has dispatched fighters. Doesn't anyone ask questions anymore?" he says a bit annoyed.

"We need to get Marcus and get out of here!" he shouts over to the colonel.

"What exactly do you think we're doing?" Colonel Winters shouts back before standing to fire his weapon again.

"There's too many, we can't take them all out!" Alex states after another shot.

"We don't need to. We just need to grab Marcus and get back to the Albatross!" he explains looking toward the control room.

"Oh is that all! And how do you propose we do that?!" Alex responds.

"Like this!" Ryland says.

Ryland quickly rises, moving around his cover and sprinting to some mangled steel structure from the ceiling. There he takes careful aim with his Sonic-Bolt and launches a powerful electric arc into a row of coolant pipes just off to the side of the aquatic soldiers' cover causing the pipes to burst and spray their contents at the attacking soldiers. Distraction in place, Ryland wastes no time.

"Hurry, go!" Ryland shouts to Alex and Colonel Winters.

They do not need to be told twice as all three quickly proceed to the control room.

Within, Marcus is tirelessly working at the computer disarming the missiles one by one, even with the flash drive Ryland gave him it is still a slow and tedious process. The codes are longer and filled with redundancies in an attempt to make them more secure. Marcus's full attention is focused on the disabling of these systems, so much so that he fails to notice Caleb regaining consciousness. Caleb gets up slowly and seeing Marcus quietly reaches into his blue jacket to pull out a regular pistol. He then comes up behind Marcus and jabs the gun in the back of his head.

"Don't move," Caleb commands causing Marcus to stop typing and slowly raise his hands.

"I thought all of you carried those electric guns," Marcus says holding his hands up.

"Those are only for the soldiers, engineers don't normally carry weapons, but I have found a pistol useful in certain situations," Caleb says in a clearly superior tone.

"Now turn around slowly," he commands backing away from Marcus.

Marcus obeys as he slowly turns around in his chair to come face to face with Caleb's gun.

"Now stand up, and move away from the panel," Caleb orders gesturing to the right with his gun.

Marcus does as he is told and moves to the right, away from the computer. Caleb moves opposite him in a circle till he is at the computer facing Marcus. With his free hand he then begins to type at the old computer. Marcus moves for an instant but a move of the gun forces him back into place.

"You know what will happen if any of those missiles launch?" Marcus asks.

"Seriously," Caleb replies looking at Marcus, "are you going to try to talk me out of it, do you honestly believe you can shake my resolve?" Caleb sarcastically answers.

"No," Marcus says placing his foot beneath an overturned chair.

"But I thought I could distract you," he claims as he suddenly kicks up the chair causing Caleb's eyes and gun to track the movement of the chair.

Seizing the opportunity Marcus grabs the gun and the two begin to wrestle for it. Caleb proves well trained and they struggle for a few moments before the gun between the two is pointed at the computer. With a smirk from Caleb two shots go off and hit the computer before Marcus is able to overpower him with an elbow to the jaw. With another punch Marcus knocks Caleb out and then rushes to the damaged computer before he even hits the ground. The screen is still functioning but the controls are damaged and sparking. Marcus tries typing at the computer but to his horror the computer is entirely unresponsive to his actions.

"No...no...come on," he says still manipulating the damaged controls. "Come on you piece of..."

However Marcus is interrupted as Ryland and his companions burst into the control room swiftly closing the door behind them. Marcus turns back to the computer and continues to work as the other three come over to him.

"Marcus we need to go!" Alex shouts coming up next to him.

"No...no!" he responds still trying to get the damaged computer to operate.

"What's wrong?" she asks looking at the screen.

"He activated four of the missiles before he shot the controls!" Marcus shouts pointing to the unconscious Caleb. "I can't get the computer to respond to stop it!" He looks at Ryland.

"Can't you turn off the computer? Or disable the system?" Colonel Winters asks.

"No," Marcus says shaking his head. "He locked the controls; a power failure will only ensure the launch."

"That sounds like Caleb all right," Ryland says looking at the screen.

"There must be something else we can do!" Alex exclaims looking at Ryland.

"Isn't there a back-up terminal or something?" she says turning back to Marcus.

"It would take too long to connect," Marcus explains.

"Well there must be something!" Colonel Winters exclaims.

"We need to get back to the Albatross," Ryland says getting their attention. "The American fighters will be here soon, and Nemo's men are—"

"Do you not get it?!" Marcus interrupts getting into Ryland's face. "Missiles are going to launch!" he shouts. "Never mind your ship, we need to figure out how to stop the launch!"

"That is what I am talking about," Ryland calmly claims.

"You mean the Albatross can stop this?" Alex asks.

"Yes, but I need to get aboard to make the modifications," he answers.

"Then let's go!" Colonel Winters exclaims moving to the back of the control room.

"There should be an emergency exit…" he begins looking around the room. "Here it is." He opens a large metal door that looks like it belongs on a submarine.

Colonel Winters walks into a room followed by the others. Dim lights come on lighting a small walkway to a ladder upon the wall which the colonel immediately starts to climb followed quickly by the others, save for Ryland who has taken out his cell phone.

"Computer, track our position and meet us when we get to ground level," he commands into the phone before ascending the ladder.

Outside the underground hangar the Albatross is swiftly turning to the left of the concrete entrance to an unassuming green hill that hides the emergency exit Colonel Winters is guiding them through. The Albatross arrives just as the grass cover exit lifts up and the four of them emerge from the hidden tunnel. No sooner have all four of them climbed out than the four cables they had used to descend from the ship come down once again. This time the bronze handles hit the ground and their sides unfasten at the top. Without a word, Ryland grabs the top of a handle which he twists to the right and slides up the cable before placing both his feet on the now open lower half on the handle. As soon as his weight is placed full upon the device he shoots up toward the opening of the Albatross.

Alex, Marcus, and Colonel Winters in turn rush to the grounded handles. Colonel Winters is the first to figure out how to twist the top of the handle free from the bottom, which he shows Alex and Marcus before stepping on the lower portion. The colonel shoots up toward the Albatross with Alex and Marcus soon to follow. They reach the top to find Ryland waiting at the controls next to the opening. Once all three step onto the ship, he turns a large dial closing the port they just entered. Colonel Winters motions to speak to Ryland but he is gone before he has the chance.

Ryland rushes to the spiral staircase and ascends only one floor, rushing into the hallway with the other three hot on his heels. This hallway is shorter than the others and has a door at its far end that automatically opens when Ryland and the others approach. It reveals the steampunk styled bomb drop housing Ryland's Anti-Particle Bomb. Ryland rushes to the bomb and opens a side panel operating some unseen controls. The other three stop in their tracks perplexed by the device in front of them, save for Alex.

"The Anti-Particle Bomb?" she asks.

The realization of what the device in front of them is enrages Colonel Winters who, in one swift motion, grabs Ryland by his collar and forces Ryland to look at him.

"What are you doing? The Nautilus is nowhere near here!" Colonel Winters shouts.

"I'm aware," Ryland says calmly freeing himself from the colonel's grip only to return to the open panel of the Anti-Particle Bomb.

"Then why are you fiddling with that thing!" Marcus shouts coming next to Ryland. "Have you forgotten? Nuclear missiles, end of the world, any of this ringing a bell?"

"Of course!!" Ryland angrily responds. "That's why I am reconfiguring the Anti-Particle Bomb to cancel out the electronics aboard the missiles!" he shouts still working at the bomb.

"This thing can stop the missiles?" Alex asks looking at the bomb.

"Yes, it will cancel out the electric fields produced by the electronics which will neutralize the missiles," he calmly explains.

"Brilliant!" Colonel Winters exclaims looking over the bomb.

"Alright Ryland!" Marcus exclaims punching the air. "Never doubted you for a second!" he states receiving an annoyed look from Ryland.

"Wait, if you use this on the missiles..." Alex begins stepping to Ryland's side. "Will you still be able to use it on the Nautilus?" she asks.

"There is more than one way to bring down the Nautilus," Ryland half-heartedly answers.

"That should do it." he says closing the panel. "Computer, as soon as the silos open launch the Anti-Particle Bomb,"

Ryland commands stepping away from the bomb with the others.

The hill soon erupts with activity as grass and dirt suddenly flies through the air revealing large missile coverings. Steam erupts from the doors as they slowly slide open and the tops of four of the newly rearmed nuclear missiles emerge from the opening ready to fire. The moment these missiles are in view the Albatross comes around and from a bottom port drops the Anti-Particle Bomb. The bomb falls in between the four nuclear missiles detonating in a brilliant flash of light, blue then a radiant white, before it hits the ground. Brief sparks of electricity surround the four missiles before the entire site goes dark.

Ryland and the others have returned to the bridge of the Albatross where Ryland takes his place at the wheel. Marcus proceeds to the window while Alex walks over to Ryland's side with the colonel not far behind.

"Missiles have been disabled," the automated voice announces.

All but Ryland send up a celebratory shout at the news, Alex patting Ryland's shoulder with a wide grin on her face. Marcus's arms are thrown up in triumph and even Colonel Winters looks pleased.

"American fighters detected," the computerized voice suddenly interrupts.

Ryland does not hesitate as he quickly turns the wheel of the Albatross while Alex and Colonel Winters back up to stay out of Ryland's way.

"Computer prepare the soft-bigboy for—" Ryland begins just as a large explosion is seen through the observatory window.

"One of the fighters has been shot down," the automated voice informs them.

"What!" Alex exclaims looking out the window.

"How?!" Colonel Winters asks Ryland.

"I didn't do anything!" Ryland says looking just as surprised as the others.

"AquaMotive is attacking the American fighters," the automated voice suddenly interjects.

"That'll work," Ryland says grabbing the wheel.

"Computer, ascend into the cloud bank and prepare to follow the—" he begins.

"We can't just fly away, we have to help them!" Alex yells grabbing Ryland's arm.

"I can't…" he begins looking Alex directly in the eye.

Ryland goes silent when he meets her fierce gaze, only to look up and see that Marcus and Colonel Winters are staring him down with similar looks.

"Right." Ryland sighs. "Computer, prepare to fire laser at AquaMotive projectiles," Ryland half-heartedly commands.

The Albatross turns around and a laser hits the next projectile aiming at the fighters. The AquaMotive rests at the far end of the hill, still firing at the American fighters while Nemo's soldiers are scrambling to get aboard. The American fighters go on the offensive and try to attack the AquaMotive. Missiles are launched from the planes but they are hit with an electrical pulse and go rearing off, falling harmlessly away from the vehicle. The fighters pass and try to circle around and attack again apparently realizing the Albatross is on their side. Before the fighters can make another pass all three suddenly explode, destroyed by missiles from an unseen source.

Colonel Winters and Marcus stare out the bridge window, a look of horror and confusion plastered upon both their faces, at the sight of the three destroyed American fighters.

"What…what happened?" Marcus asks turning to look at Ryland.

"Computer, what happened?" Ryland asks.

"American fighters attacked from an external source out of my sensor range," the automated voice answers.

"The Nautilus," he realizes. "Crap! Computer, ascend, ascend now!" he says flipping some switches next to the wheel.

"What—" Alex begins to ask.

She is interrupted as the Albatross is physically rocked to its side sending all them crashing to the floor. Warning sirens begin going off in the control room as Ryland scrabbles to the wheel while the ship is still trying to steady itself. Ryland manages to get hold of the wheel only to have the ship violently rock to the side again. Alex and the others are not as lucky as once again they are sent to the floor.

"The Nautilus is attacking!" Ryland shouts at the wheel. "Computer, get the camouflage sensor back online now!" Ryland commands.

"Sensors reactivating in 20 seconds," the automated voice responds.

"In 20 seconds we'll be dead!" Alex states managing to stand and brace herself against a panel.

"Can't you go any faster?" Marcus asks getting to his feet as well.

"No I cannot, Marcus," the automated voice answers.

"I thought you were good with computers," Alex says looking over at Marcus.

"Not ones that can talk!" he shouts as the Albatross rocks to the side yet again.

"Could you two try to act like soldiers for one second?" Colonel Winters commands holding onto the door frame.

Without warning the Albatross suddenly stabilizes itself, the warning sirens going off all at once. Ryland looks around the room still clutching the wheel as Marcus, Alex, and the colonel begin to stand upright without gripping the ship itself.

"What?" Marcus asks going over to the window.

"Why did it stop?" Alex asks Ryland.

"I don—" Ryland begins before suddenly looking up toward the ceiling.

"Computer where is the AquaMotive?!" Ryland shouts.

"The AquaMotive is out of the range of my sensors," the automated voice responds.

"Of course," Ryland quietly says clenching his fists.

"Sensors detect incoming American fighters," the automated voice announces.

"And us with four dead American fighters," he says returning to the wheel.

"Computer, start scanning for the Nautilus once we get over the Atlantic Ocean," Ryland commands.

Chapter Seven
The Young Game

The Albatross ascends into the clouds before its camouflage capabilities activate and the ship takes on the appearance of the sky. The trip is uneventful and quiet with only the computerized voice interrupting to inform Ryland that there is no mention of the Albatross over secured military channels. Ryland remains at the wheel of the ship staring straight ahead through the observatory window. Despite foiling Nemo's plans Ryland bears a defeated look upon his face and has not spoken since his last command to the computer. Marcus, Alex, and Colonel Winters have retreated just a few feet behind Ryland unsure of what their next move should be. They remain silent until Alex steps cautiously forward toward Ryland.

"Well, we stopped World War III, that's something right?" she cautiously asks him.

"Nemo will not give up so easily," he answers keeping his eyes forward. "As long as he is out there he's a threat."

"So what's our next move?" Marcus asks.

"My next move is to find a safe place to drop the three of you off," Ryland answers receiving looks of disbelief from all three of them.

"Then I go after the Nautilus and Nemo," Ryland coldly states.

"You're just going to drop us off?" Alex indignantly asks. "After all of this?"

"Captain, you saw what happened today," Colonel Winters interjects. "You can't honestly still believe you can do this alone?" He comes over to stand by Alex.

"Yeah come on man, were just starting to get along," Marcus says patting Ryland on the back.

"Is there somewhere in particular you would like to be dropped off?" Ryland responds.

"Ryland you can't just—" Alex begins to interject.

"Nautilus spotted off the shore of Alghero, Italy a couple of hours ago," the automated voice interrupts.

"Italy?" Ryland responds looking over to a nearby panel.

"Why was he in Italy?" he asks walking past the three soldiers to the panel.

"Insufficient data, an attack on CERN in Switzerland was reported while

Nemo's soldiers were in South Dakota," the computerized voice answers.

"CERN?" Ryland asks looking up toward the ceiling. "Why would he attack there, was anything stolen?"

"Unconfirmed," the automated voice responds.

"Call coming in from the Nautilus," the automated voice suddenly announces.

All three of the American soldiers immediately look up at the ceiling in absolute disbelief, before turning to Ryland who is unaffected by the news. Marcus motions to speak but no words are formed as Alex and Colonel Winters just stare at Ryland sharing the same bewildered look. Ryland looks at the three of them for a moment before walking past them to a maintenance panel at the far end of the bridge.

"Put him on screen two," Ryland commands.

Ryland reaches the panel as Alex, Colonel Winters, and Marcus all gather around Ryland. The bewildered look is still plastered upon their faces as the screen comes alive and the face of captain Nemo is staring back at them. Immediately their expression changes from bewildered to determined and angry. Nemo who is sitting in his office gives a look of surprise at the three soldiers gathered around Ryland before turning his gaze back on his friend with a smirk on his face.

"Nemo, this is a surprise," Ryland says in a monotone tone.

"Not as surprising as you," he answers scanning the trio again. "Since when do you have a crew?"

"We're from the base you attacked!" Alex angrily interjects.

"Survivors!" Nemo answers clearly surprised. "Or should I say stowaways, what do you think Ryland?" he says in a playful tone.

"They're not staying," Ryland calmly answers.

"Very good," Nemo answers. "Though I'm surprised you let them on at all, but that does explain things, I knew you'd never help that submarine voluntarily."

"What do you want?" Colonel Winters demands, doing his best to keep his military composure.

"Your stowaways don't seem to know their place Ryland," Nemo sneers. "At least your ancestor made it clear where his stowaways stood."

"Enough, Nemo," Ryland says still in a monotone voice. "Your attempt at starting World War III is sunk and the

Nautilus will follow soon." His face remains expressionless.

"That's right!" Marcus exclaims.

"Come now Ryland, you're better than that!" Nemo responds with a light chuckle.

"I assume you've heard about my trip to CERN," he sneers. "So what do you think?" Nemo asks in a taunting tone.

"You've always had a fondness for Swiss chocolate," Ryland replies.

"Ha, ha, ha!" Nemo laughs a little too loudly. "Ryland, Ryland, Ryland, honestly how do you hope to beat me," he asks in a taunting tone.

"I admit you won the day, but I knew you would, I know you Ryland, I know exactly how smart you are and I know your shortcomings…" he continues. "It was once my full-time job to point them out."

"Get to the point Nemo!" Ryland says a bit aggravated.

"The point? How many games of chess did we play Ryland? And despite your superior intelligence you could never beat me, not once, and do you know why?" Nemo asks in a taunting tone.

"Why do I feel you're going to tell me no matter what I answer?" Ryland says returning to his monotone tone.

"Because you could only see what was right in front of you, you could never play the long game. I'm playing the long game, Ryland, you may have captured my knight, but in twelve moves I'll have checkmate," Nemo states in a taunting tone.

"This isn't chess, I'm not bound by rules Nemo," Ryland replies.

"Of course you are!" Nemo exclaims. "You're not doing this because you care, you're doing this because you want to prove that you're not Robur the Conqueror.

"And that makes you weak. If Robur the Conqueror was hunting me I would have been in chains by now," Nemo states.

"You'll never get the chance to be in chains!" Colonel Winters angrily exclaims.

"We'll just have to see about that," Nemo answers with a smirk. "Because you're wrong Ryland. This is a game of chess, winner take all, the board set, the game young." His tone is mocking. "The next move is yours; choose wisely my dear friend."

With that, the screen goes black leaving our three soldiers with many questions...

About Scott Strozier

Scott Strozier has a Bachelor's degree in Electrical Power and Engineering Technology and is currently working as a Technician in the Blood Bank at the American Red Cross, as well as a part time artist and writer. The subjects of his stories are not bound to any genre but focus on conveying a message or moral in an interesting way that will not bore the reader but get them to consider how the message is to be received. Like his stories his interests and hobbies are diverse and include various martial arts, history, mysteries, true crime and weapons design.

Social Media

Facebook:
https://www.facebook.com/howard.hughes.5621

Archinect:
https://archinect.com/LDVsketches

Saatchi Art:
https://www.saatchiart.com/davinci221

Fine Art America:
https://fineartamerica.com/profiles/scott-strozier.html

Amazon:
https://www.amazon.com/Political-Demons-Scott-Strozier-ebook/dp/B01FWGH0F4

Rise Art:
https://www.riseart.com/artist/scott-strozier